"Have you ever made love in a balloon?"

Even as she spoke, Nicole felt her cheeks flush. But the warmth of Adam's breath in her ear sent desire searing through her, and she was glad she'd asked.

"Never," he murmured. "I'd probably lose control and crash."

Here, floating in this sun-drenched heaven, all Nicole's inhibitions drifted away. "Trust me," she whispered. "You'll be perfectly safe." She slid her hands up his arms and eased off his jacket. Silently she unbuttoned his shirt.

Adam leaned back against the gondola, moaning softly as her palms moved over his bare chest, then traveled lower. He was suddenly more than willing to share command of this particular flight....

Elaine K. Stirling admires people who take chances and stand out from the crowd. Her characters in *Almost Heaven* share the risky pleasure of ballooning. Elaine was inspired to write their story after reading about the first Atlantic crossing in a helium balloon.

Elaine has had her share of adventures, too, having traveled all over the world. She's now living in Toronto with her two sons and has launched a promising career as a Harlequin author.

Books by Elaine K. Stirling

HARLEQUIN INTRIGUE
28–UNSUSPECTED CONDUCT
35–MIDNIGHT OBSESSION
53–FOUL PLAY

Almost Heaven

ELAINE K. STIRLING

Harlequin Books

TORONTO • NEW YORK • LONDON
AMSTERDAM • PARIS • SYDNEY • HAMBURG
STOCKHOLM • ATHENS • TOKYO • MILAN

To my father, Oliver Maki,
for instilling perseverance and
the courage to take risks.

Published January 1987

ISBN 0-373-25239-0

1

THEY WERE like giant India-rubber balls held captive in mid-bounce. Nicole scanned the field of gas balloons glistening in the morning sun. The colossal orbs created a vibrant display of crimson and daffodil, azure and lavender, stripes and spots and mythical figures rearing and straining against their tethers. A west wind fluttered by, taunting the ebony tendrils that escaped Nicole's braid, but she pushed her hair away impatiently and frowned as a familiar prickle of excitement skittered along her nerve endings.

Not now, Cole, she told herself firmly. This was not the time for an anxiety attack. She had to come across as cool and decisive if she was going to persuade a total stranger to take her on as his copilot.

What was his name again? Cole bent down to pick up her duffel bag then slung it over one shoulder. Bigfoot? No . . . Blackfoot. That was it. Too bad she'd forgotten to ask Warren what his friend's first name was.

By now, a sea of spectators had flooded the launch site, further complicating Cole's attempt to locate this Blackfoot fellow. She paused several times to scan the crowd but saw only observers, their faces agog. At last, though, a blade of logic poked its head through Cole's quandary and she smiled.

All she had to do was find the balloon and, in all likelihood, the pilot would not be far away. Luckily, Warren's description of *Stargrazer* had been accurate, if a little understated, and Cole soon spotted her at the end of the field. A gigantic indigo sphere with an arc of silver stars reaching skyward, she was magnificent; all the other balloons looked slightly garish in comparison.

Cole approached *Stargrazer* and spotted a man balanced high on the edge of the wicker gondola, inspecting the rigging. His back was toward Cole, who took the opportunity to appreciate the masculine strength in his broad shoulders. Somewhat taller than average, he was solidly built, the interplay of powerful muscles evident beneath his navy T-shirt as he worked the nylon ropes leading to the load ring.

There wasn't a trace of excess flesh at his waist and hips. Nor, Cole noted with a faint shudder, was there any of that familiar sag of the buttocks that plagued so many of her male coworkers, a fact explicitly enunciated by the lean cut of his khaki slacks. All in all, his body was concise and spare—the ideal masculine composition.

Involuntarily, Cole smiled as her eyes moved upward to take in his well-shaped head. His hair was a mass of close-cropped brown curls, which the sun danced off with sparks of gilt auburn. What she wouldn't give to have curls like that!

"Mr. Blackfoot?" she inquired finally, her initial curiosity sated. Obviously, he was much too intent on his task to have noticed her arrival.

He turned.

When his eyes met hers, Cole felt her heart thump against her chest. He might just as well have been faceless for all the attention she paid his other features. It was impossible to notice anything beyond those eyes—hazel or emerald or whatever they were. Colors passed across them as swiftly as the high cumulus clouds overhead scudded across the sun. One second they were as fathomless as a wooded pond in spring, the next as turbulent as a summer tempest.

Green, she decided finally. They had to be green when they were in a state of tranquillity... if they ever were.

"The name is Blackfoot," he said in a husky voice. "Not mister, just Blackfoot."

"Oh, I see. Sorry." Cole would have offered her hand to introduce herself properly, but he stood some four feet above her and would have had to stoop. Somehow, he didn't look to be in the mood for stooping. "I'm Cole Jameson," she said, her fingers curling around the strap of her duffel bag defensively. "I'm your new copilot."

She could have sworn she saw a flicker of amusement dispel his wariness for an instant, but it was gone as quickly as it appeared. Instead, he knit together a pair of thick dark brows; and a mouth that, under other circumstances, might have been described as gentle turned down in an expression of overt annoyance. "I think you've made some kind of mistake," he growled. "I already have a copilot...even though he's two hours late."

"Yes, I know. That's Warren Sanders; he won't be coming." Feeling a hint of courage returning to her voice, Cole pressed on. "He threw his back out this morning trying to move his fridge. He'll be flat on the floor for days."

Blackfoot didn't say a word, yet suddenly Cole was overwhelmed by an irrational urge to back away and hightail it out of there as quickly as she could. Not that premature retreats were her usual style, but she had never before been on the receiving end of green eyes whose owner was obviously about to boil over.

"I—I'd have been here sooner," she stammered, willing her feet to stay put, "but it was already after dawn when Warren phoned, and then I got stuck in traffic..." Why was she apologizing, for heaven's sake? She was doing both of them a favor by being here at all, and on very short notice.

"Well, that's just great!" declared Blackfoot, leaping down effortlessly from the gondola. "Just blasted great!"

He stood half a head higher than Cole, but his closeness made him seem much taller. His features were deep-set, rugged, with the sienna tones of an outdoor man. He had a high forehead, a chin that was obstinately square and cleft and lines that ran from the sides of his nose to the corners of his mouth. He might have been hand hewn from Appalachian hardwood, except for the snapping vitality of his eyes and those curls that lent him an air of rakish youthfulness. It was hard to tell his age by looking at him, but Warren had said he knew him from college, so he'd be fortyish, eight or nine years older than Cole.

"I see I've arrived too late to help with the inflation," she ventured with a determined grin. She really didn't blame him for being upset. "Is everything ready for lift-off?"

Blackfoot was beginning to look distinctly uncomfortable. "Look, Ms...uh, Jameson, it was nice of Warren to send out a replacement, and you'd certainly make an attractive addition to the balloon, but this is an important race. I'm not about to risk the outcome by having an amateur aboard."

"Wait just a minute. I happen to be a fine balloonist!" Cole protested, indignation deepening the color in her cheeks. Or was it, she wondered, a reaction to Blackfoot's blatant assessment of her body? She wasn't immune to the flattery of an admiring glance, but he was giving her much more than the usual once-over. His glinting eyes intently followed the lines of her slim-fitting white-cotton jump suit, which was now chafing her flushed skin like burlap. It didn't help matters when an ill-timed breath of cool air feathered by, causing Blackfoot's descending gaze to come screeching to a halt somewhere around her midsection and slide back up with staggering boldness to her breasts.

An eternity later, he lifted thick auburn lashes to convey the satisfied look of a man who knows he possesses the psychological edge. "How often have you flown helium balloons?"

Damn! He would have to pick up on that right away. "I . . . uh, I'm familiar with the principles of helium ballooning, even though I've only flown hot air. I'm nearly ready to do my solo flight."

Blackfoot scratched his chin with a large, square hand. "Very impressive, Ms Jameson, and I wish you luck. Unfortunately, there's no room on this rig for a theorist on gas ballooning."

That did it, there was a fine line between being understandably cautious and unreasonably pigheaded. Blackfoot had just crossed the line. "A balloon is a balloon, Mr., er, Blackfoot! Heat makes it rise, the lack of same makes it fall; wind is its only source of directional power and—"

"All right, all right!" Blackfoot raised his hands in surrender.

"—and I'm not afraid to show you what I can do." There. Cole always felt better when she finished a sentence. Blackfoot was regarding her with such intensity she was almost sure she had him persuaded. Well, that hadn't been so bad after all, she thought with a dash of swagger; she had expected worse.

"Okay," he said evenly, pausing to look at his watch. "We have twenty minutes to lift-off. That should be just about enough time to brief you and get you settled into the chase car."

Cole's duffel bag fell to the ground with an incredulous thunk. "Chase car!" she ground out between clenched teeth. "I did not drive over fifty miles on my Saturday morning to follow your stupid balloon around the backwoods of Pennsylvania! You could've gotten any half-witted ninny to do that!" She bent down to recover her bag then tossed it past Blackfoot into *Stargrazer*'s gondola. Proof physical that she intended to win this argument. "I promised a friend I'd fill in for him," she continued determinedly, "and that is what I'm going to do."

Freed of the duffel bag, Cole planted her feet firmly apart and placed her fists on her hips. What did it matter that the man could probably pick her up and propel her ten feet in the air if he wanted to? Just let him try!

Their eyes locked in isometric rage and it was all Cole could do to keep from flinching. The prospect of sharing confined quarters with some hothead was not particularly appealing to her right now, but this was hardly the time to say she'd changed her mind. If only he'd do something other than glare.

Blackfoot, instead of affording Cole the satisfaction of a retort, simply turned on one heel and resumed his task of adjusting the rigging.

So he was just going to pretend she didn't exist. Well, he would soon learn that Cole Jameson was capable of matching him tactic for tactic. Sooner or later, one of them was going to wear down, and Cole decided it wasn't going to be her. "Look, Blackfoot," she began guardedly, wondering at the edge of her argument where he had picked up such a name, "I'm going up there with you. We can either waste the next twenty minutes arguing, at the end of which there will be a horrendous scene while you attempt to toss me out of the gondola, or you can accept the fact that I'm copiloting and give me a rundown on the use of ballast, the proposed flight plan and your navigational techniques."

Cole had been projecting her measured ultimatum directly at a knot of pulsing muscle at the base of Blackfoot's neck. As if in response, she saw the muscle begin to relax, smoothing out beneath the sun-darkened skin.

Blackfoot turned and coolly leveled his green eyes on her. One corner of his mouth lifted, but whether it was a sneer or a smile Cole couldn't be sure. Still, something told her that Blackfoot in his taciturn way was acknowledging her victory.

Much to her dismay, however, she felt no flush of triumph, only a quiver of trepidation. Intuition told her Blackfoot had relented only so that she'd have to prove her mettle aloft. If she'd been exaggerating her ballooning skills, it would soon become painfully evident at five thousand feet.

"Welcome aboard, mate," Blackfoot said, his craggy face expressionless as he held out his strong square hand. When Cole took it, her own hand suddenly seemed dwarfed, defenseless and clammy. Judging from Blackfoot's cool dry palms, preflight jitters weren't part of the man's repertoire. Then he released his grip and Cole felt a twinge of something reminiscent of regret. For goodness' sake, what more had she hoped for: a kiss on the palm?

Blackfoot stepped back and turned to look up at the balloon, resting one sinewy forearm against the gondola. It was clear from his expression and from the way he touched *Stargrazer* that he loved her the way a captain loves his ship, and suddenly Cole wished she hadn't been so pushy. She could understand his reluctance to have a stranger on board, intruding on the matchless tranquillity of flight. But she also knew it was difficult to fly a helium balloon alone, much less win a race solo.

Somewhat incongruously, her eyes flicked across the web of brown hair that covered Blackfoot's forearm. It looked soft and silky, in marked contrast to the iron muscles underneath.

"First, the rules of the race," he began in tones much less condemnatory than before. The huskiness was still there, though, a gruff bristly edge that was almost sensuous now that the threat of anger was removed. "It's a pilot-declared goal. I've charted a probable northeast flight path of one hundred miles. Our target is just south of the Poconos."

"Is there a time limit?" Cole asked, conscious of the preflight adrenaline coursing through her veins.

"Six hours, but we're judged solely on how close we come to our target. I've estimated five hours of flight time, and so far it looks like the weather's going to cooperate."

"Have you worked out a ballasting sequence?" She detected a snippet of respect in the far reaches of Blackfoot's eyes.

"Not precisely, but we shouldn't have to ballast before five thousand feet, and if the westerlies hold out, we should be able to maintain that altitude. There's plenty of sand aboard, but I'd like to use as little as possible while the sun's high in case we encounter katabatic winds in the foothills."

"Then maybe," Cole suggested, swallowing a smile with considerable effort, "we ought to climb higher before we reach the hills, and we might avoid the downdrafts altogether." *Nice try, Blackfoot, but big words won't scare me off either.*

His green eyes zeroed in with maddening ambivalence and studied her. "Maybe you've got something there. We'll see how it goes." He held out his hand. "Shall we climb aboard?"

Cole hesitated briefly, struggling against the fundamental instinct of fear. It angered her, this lack of courage, and no matter how many times she flew, it always threatened to take over. But she'd never give up ballooning and the sensation of freedom it gave her. As long as she steeled herself against fear, she knew she would never become what her ex-husband had accused her of being.

She slipped her hand into Blackfoot's and their fingers folded over each other's palms. Incredibly, a current as vital as electricity passed between them. Cole lifted her eyes to the man, and it seemed as though they were no longer strangers but kindred spirits, united in their imminent battle with the elements. She didn't have to prove herself to Blackfoot; he understood her passion for the sport because he loved it just as much as she did. Suddenly, she was very glad she had come.

The wicker gondola was typically small but well-organized, with narrow benches and storage beneath. Cole watched Blackfoot as he scanned the interior. There was a certain sensitivity in his face that became apparent the longer she watched him, as if here in the balloon he felt safe and willing to let his guard down. Cole knew that feeling well.

Blackfoot's physique was flawless, and his face—if not exactly handsome—was sentient, alive, expressive. He was a man who would age well. The lines would become etched a little deeper, the curls would thin but his face would always register an indomitable strength of character.

"You check the instruments," he issued succinctly, in a tone befitting the one in command. "I'll secure the drag line."

"Roger."

"Don't forget to set the variometer—"

"To zero," Cole interjected, smiling. "I know."

Blackfoot tossed a grin over his shoulder. "Just testing."

Several hundred Boy Scouts, whose jamboree coincided with the ballooning event, comprised the ground crew. At the issuance of an order from the race officials, the boys clambered to their assigned places, some untying tethers, others using their collective weight to hold down the straining balloons.

"We're third to lift off," Blackfoot said while they watched the first balloon make ready to launch.

"*Stargrazer* is really beautiful," Cole said, the tingle of nerves bringing out a need to chatter. "She's so much more striking than all the other balloons."

Blackfoot merely grunted, his mind apparently on items less aesthetic than the external finery of balloons. He turned to Cole. "You do know the difference between the vent line and the rip line, don't you?"

She gave him a deliberately blank look but wiped it off her face when she saw his look of alarm. "Don't worry, I do," she assured him. "If I pull this red cord, our descent will be much more sudden than we bargained for. Believe me, Blackfoot, my sense of self-preservation is just as strong as yours."

Blackfoot laughed for the first time, a deep, relaxed sound. "Sorry. I hadn't expected a stranger for a copilot, and it makes me feel better to know you can find your way around in here." When a signal from the judges indicated the second balloon had cleared, Blackfoot was once again all business. "All right...ready!" he called to the group of Scouts. "Hands off...launch!"

Within a hairbreadth of a second, *Stargrazer* responded to his command. The balloon shivered slightly, freeing herself from the unwanted fetters, and then she began to climb.

"All clear below," Cole said as her eyes swept the perimeter for signs of entangled ropes and lingering spectators.

"Good," Blackfoot returned, his eyes studying the instruments. "Everything's registering normally...a good steady lift-off." He straightened and brought himself next to Cole in a single stride, his arm coming around her shoulder in a gesture that felt totally natural. "Spectacular, isn't it?" he said, now ready to share the simple beauty of the sport.

Their eyes came together; they held, and Cole experienced a splendid rush of emotion as she swam in the clear green depths of his gaze. "It is spectacular," she whispered, discovering something in his eyes that could compete even with the flawless magnificence of a balloon in flight. It took all the willpower she could muster to tear her gaze away.

Below them were the lush greens of early summer, the rich and rolling farmland, the forests, the azure sky radiant beyond. The clouds were marshmallow puffs and too distant to intrude on *Stargrazer*'s flight. As the cheers of the crowd began to ebb, Cole experienced a sense of growing peace. It felt as though they were suspended motionless in a sphere of celestial tranquillity. Blackfoot's arm was still around her; she liked how it felt.

But all too soon he pulled away and moved to the panel of instruments behind them. "We're approaching four thousand feet with a slight pull to the north," he said, but it seemed as though he was talking more to himself than to Cole. She realized with a sudden pang that he probably could have flown *Stargrazer* alone, and she wondered why he hadn't come right out and told her so from the start. It wasn't that he made her feel like an intruder—she felt quite comfortable with him— but she sensed a restless streak of maverick and suspected that, like her, he cherished his solitude.

"We're at forty-two hundred feet...forty-five," Blackfoot continued, "slowing down...forty-eight hundred feet. Aha! We've stabilized and didn't even have to touch the ballast."

"Wonderful!" exclaimed Cole. She lifted her eyes to the base of the balloon. "I can't believe the silence in a helium balloon. No roar of propane, no whoosh of hot air. It seems almost too easy."

Blackfoot smiled. "Don't let it fool you. The winds like to lull us into a false sense of complacency before flipping us into a rotor or two." He lowered himself to a wicker bench. "We should be all right for a while, though—I hope."

Cole returned his grin, her spirits riding as high as the rest of her. She couldn't bring herself to sit down; there was too much to see, even though the Pennsylvania countryside was totally familiar to her. She never seemed to tire of the magic of soaring above reality, now laying below them like an innocent toy land.

She knew that Blackfoot was watching her as she looked out over the side of the gondola, but she felt more flattered than self-conscious. She had already taken more than a few peeks herself while his concentration had been elsewhere, and she had to admit she liked what she'd seen.

"How did you get a name like that?" Blackfoot asked suddenly, slicing into her frivolous daydream.

Cole turned to look at him, perplexed. "Who...me?"

Blackfoot pretended to look for someone else. "Of course, you! Who else could I be talking to? Were you named after anthracite or the color of your hair?"

"Neither," Cole answered with a laugh. "It's spelled C-O-L-E, not C-O-A-L, and it's short for Nicole. My grandmother was a Cajun, hence the French name and the black hair."

"Hmm...Cole," he mused. "I like it, sort of no-nonsense. It suits you."

"How about you?" Cole asked, recalling the fitting adage about a pot calling a kettle black.

"How about me what?" he asked evenly, his long legs eased out in front of him and his hands folded over his taut stomach.

"Your name! How'd you get it? Except for your complexion, you don't look particularly Indian."

"I'm not," he admitted. "Beneath this windburn lies a true Irish paleface. I was raised in Montana on a Blackfoot reservation where my father was a doctor. When we moved back east, I picked up the nickname and it stuck."

"Really? Well, yours suits you, too, oddly enough. What's your real name?"

Blackfoot shrugged. "I don't use it much." He turned brusquely and leaned forward to read the variometer. "Damn, we're descending. We're down to four thousand feet."

Cole looked up, shielding her eyes. "It must be that cloud that just moved over the sun. Looks like it'll be with us for a while." She slid him a quizzical glance. "Shall we ballast?"

"Not yet. Wait and see." They watched the instrument panel together, mentally ticking off the seconds. "We're still falling," Blackfoot said at last. "Go ahead and cut open a sand bag."

Cole sliced across one of the burlap bags that hung over the gondola's side, letting the fine grains spill into the air. "Are we rising yet?" she asked. There were no feelings of vertigo in a balloon; it was like gliding along a giant, invisible surf.

"Yeah, it doesn't take much." He paused. "Okay, that should do it." He came to her side. "Let me haul that bag in here so it doesn't leak."

The strength of Blackfoot's arm moved against Cole's as they dragged the gunnysack into the gondola. She could feel the flex of his muscles against her skin and the silky brown hair tickled her forearm; a delicious shiver ran through Cole's entire body. Oxygen deprivation, she told herself bracingly.

Still disoriented, Cole moved away and turned to look at the gauges. "We're at five thousand feet now . . . and holding."

Blackfoot didn't answer. His eyes were scanning the horizon, his thoughts a million miles farther. She watched him for a moment and wondered what had distracted him so. Whatever it was, she had an idea you'd have to peel back a lot of layers to reach it. Shrugging, she turned her attention to their flight path. "Oh, look, Blackfoot, there's Hopewell Village!"

She pointed at the northern horizon where the restored nineteenth-century village had come into view, idyllic and picturesque. They could easily pick out the blacksmith shop, the schoolhouse and the general store. The silence of the panorama was punctuated only by the barking of a dog, which was no doubt aware of the silent aeronautical intruder.

"Terrific," said Blackfoot. "We're making good time." His green eyes passed over the scene with satisfaction and he smiled. Cole noticed a tiredness around his eyes; not the type one gets from lack of sleep, but the deeper kind, a fatigue that starts on the inside. Yet when he smiled, the weariness seemed to go away. She wished he would smile more often.

"How long have you been an aeronaut, Blackfoot?"

"About ten, twelve years."

"Have you always flown helium?"

Blackfoot shook his head and ran his hand along the rigging. "I started with hot air like most people do, I guess, but once I got a taste of these beauties, I was hooked." He might have been carrying on small talk, but it was obvious his real contentment lay with *Stargrazer*'s flawless performance.

"What do you do for a living?" Cole asked, deciding to try a different tack.

"I don't work."

Cole had prepared herself for an odd answer: lumberjack or stevedore or railroad navvy. Any one of those replies wouldn't have surprised her; such occupations suited him somehow. "It must be difficult to maintain a hobby like this. I mean, the helium, the maintenance..."

"It's worth the trouble," he replied, as if that explained everything.

Cole brushed back a fringe of hair from her eyes. The man certainly didn't spend a lot of energy on words. She sat down on a wicker bench and wondered how to get through the next few hours, deciding she'd even settle for a storm...anything other than dragging conversation out of this Blackfoot person.

Blackfoot turned to her suddenly. "How do you know Warren?"

Cole lifted her sky-blue eyes in surprise. So he was capable of something as base as curiosity. She struggled with the temptation to mutter something equally cryptic, but decided that was a bit childish. Everyone was entitled to his personality, after all. "We both work at the same advertising agency."

His mouth turned up in a smile. "Oh, yeah? Are you a secretary, or one of those hard-bitten, high-powered executive types?"

Cole had to laugh at his deliberate lack of subtlety. "Let's just say I can't type worth beans."

"I figured as much. You don't strike me as the type who takes orders well."

Was she imagining the thread of sarcasm in his voice, or was it her usual defensive reaction to people who mistook the external image for the real Cole Jameson? "I know what you mean," she said, feeling a little abashed. "Just because I did such a thorough job of buffaloing my way on board this morning."

"Your methods are effective," he admitted, but his chuckle told her he wasn't being critical. That suddenly seemed important to her.

"Believe me, it's all surface bluster. I've gotten into the habit of using tactics like this at work, but it never seems to get any easier with practice."

Blackfoot leaned back against the side of the gondola, his elbows hooked over the edge. His eyes seemed to reach deep inside and Cole got the feeling she'd never really fooled him for a minute.

"So why work in advertising?" he asked.

To anyone else, Cole would have tossed off a quip about the money or the challenge or the lure of competitiveness. She never would have said, "I have to, or I might revert back to being the doormat I was for ten years." The confession had slipped out before she had a chance to edit it.

Blackfoot raised his eyebrows quizzically. "You, a doormat? That's hard to believe."

"It wouldn't be if you knew my husband," she blurted, wondering why she wasn't curling up inside with embarrassment. A woman never talked about a previous marriage to a man she had just met unless she was deliberately trying to get rid of him. Poor Blackfoot was something of a captive audience, but probably considered boredom an insufficient cause to jump overboard.

"You're married," he stated flatly.

Cole shook her head. "Not any more."

"Sorry, didn't mean to pry."

It was amazing, but he really did sound apologetic. Sensitivity was such a rare virtue, it was hard to recognize when it actually surfaced. "It's all right," Cole said, smiling. "Being a divorcée fits the professional image. Ad execs don't go home and cook tuna casseroles and sort socks. We're expected to entertain clients six nights a week and be in tune with the latest fitness craze and buy our groceries in trendy little gourmet shops."

"Is that what you do?" Blackfoot asked, gently teasing.

"Hardly," returned Cole, lifting her hands hopelessly, "but at least I don't have to sort socks anymore."

A sudden chill in the air brought them back to the immediacy of the race. Looking up, they saw a large, gray-rimmed cumulus cloud blocking the sun's rays; the instruments were already registering an alarming rate of descent.

"Blast it," muttered Blackfoot. He checked the compass and did some quick calculations in his log. "We're still heading almost due north; if we climb higher maybe we can find an air current heading east."

They jettisoned the remainder of the open sandbag and the entire contents of a second one before they found a west wind. With remarkable ease, *Stargrazer* settled into her new flight path and the crew relaxed.

"Are you warm enough?" Blackfoot asked, staring at the goosebumps speckling Cole's forearms.

"I have a jacket in my bag." She sounded much calmer than she felt. Not that they'd really been in any danger, but the trip had been so peaceful till now—almost mesmerizing—that the sudden spurt of activity had rattled her. "Are you hungry?" she asked after donning a windbreaker. "I packed us a lunch."

A smile of appreciation lit Blackfoot's craggy face. "You're an angel of mercy, Cole. Warren was supposed to have done that."

"Good. Well, we might as well eat now before we hit those old katabatics, right?" Blackfoot's mulish grin confirmed Cole's earlier suspicion that he'd been testing her, but it didn't matter. Their mutual swords seemed to be sheathed for the moment.

They munched on sandwiches and fruit and watched the rolling countryside below grow more dramatic. Farmlands gave way to dense forests, meandering rivers and the ancient foothills of the Appalachians. It occurred to Cole that despite the occasional hazards of flying at such heights, she was enjoying herself immensely. Never having competed in a race before, she'd anticipated this day as providing all the enjoyment of a bombing mission. And she'd definitely had misgivings about spending so many hours with a stranger in an airborne space smaller than most elevators.

"Are you seeing anyone?" Blackfoot asked after crunching into a juicy Granny Smith apple.

Cole wondered where he'd picked up the habit of firing questions as though they were heat-seeking missiles. It was virtually impossible to dodge them gracefully. "Not really."

"Does that mean yes?"

"It means no."

"And Warren?"

"Just friends." Cole bit into her apple and met his bold gaze. "What about you?"

Blackfoot gave an off-hand wave. "Warren and I are just friends, too." They both laughed.

Blackfoot finished his lunch and got to his feet, whereupon every trace of rational thought flew right out of Cole's head. Like filings to a magnet, her eyes were drawn down the length of Blackfoot's torso to his taut stomach, narrow hips and the low masculine ride of his khaki slacks.

It had to be the altitude that was making her normally systematic mind spin out of control like this. In all her years of flying, Cole had never even considered seduction on board a balloon, yet she was acutely conscious of the nearness of Blackfoot's body.

Hoping that busywork would alter her train of thought, Cole brushed the crumbs from her lap and proceeded to clean up the remains of their lunch. Her heart was racing in the thin, cool air and Blackfoot's green-eyed gaze was as palpable as a touch. "How much farther, do you suppose, until we reach our target?" she asked with feigned nonchalance.

Blackfoot, an obvious master of stoicism, continued his perusal of her and said, "At the rate we're flying, I'd guess about an hour. The target is a small farm near Ashfield. You can't miss it—there's a windmill at one end and white picket fencing."

Suddenly, violently, as though they had been kicked by a giant, unseen foot, the gondola lurched out from beneath the balloon, and jerked back. Cole would have crashed into the instrument panel—or worse—if Blackfoot had not caught her in time. He braced her body with his arms, one gripping her shoulders, the other encircling her waist. His mouth drew near her ear and he murmured soft reassurances to her.

Gradually, the terror that had wrenched Cole's stomach into knots eased and her wildly thumping heart slowed to a strong, steady rhythm that matched the pulse of the man who held her. She felt herself lean into his strength and draw from it as if from a well.

"Are you all right?" Blackfoot's voice was husky against Cole's ear. She could smell the pine scent of his after-shave and feel his weather-roughened cheek next to hers. Those sensations were as soothing as his words.

"I'm okay," she rasped, lifting her eyes to his face. He looked so calm, so sure of himself, Cole had the inane thought that he could make anything unpleasant go away. Then her eyes fell to his mouth, scant inches from hers. It was a gentle mouth, the lower lip full and inviting. Cole wondered whether their mouths were moving closer together or if it was the distant clouds sailing in the background that made her think so. And if it was only an illusion, if he really wasn't going to kiss her, then why was she letting it bother her? Blackfoot was pulling away from her now, his arms dropping to his sides as he turned to check the altimeter.

"A wind shear," he stated flatly. "We won't run into too many of those."

Cole nodded, trying to shake herself free of lingering disappointment. There had been no episode of intimacy. She had only imagined it—an aeronautical variation of shell shock. "So what do we do now?" she asked, hoping Blackfoot wouldn't notice the lack of enthusiasm in her voice.

"For starters, we change our course. That little encounter knocked us into a northerly current. We'll try flying below it."

Blackfoot took hold of the vent line and pulled, releasing some of the balloon's helium into the atmosphere. The immense indigo sphere slackened visibly, creaking in protest, but as her pilot released the line *Stargrazer* responded and adjusted to her new capacity.

Flying closer to the ground than they had for the entire flight, they could hear sounds drifting upward as clearly as if they had been strolling along the rural roads. They were flying toward a farmhouse, its lack of paint visible even at two thousand feet, when they heard the acrimonious tone of a woman shrieking, "Harold! Harold, get out here this minute!"

There was a moment of silence then the slam of a squeaky porch door. "Yes, Agnes?" came the reply.

"Didn't I tell you to fix this front step? My whole foot went right through it!"

Poor Harold's defense went unheard as *Stargrazer* drifted past, though Agnes's voice followed them for some time with the shrillness of a smoke detector.

Waves of laughter rose in Cole's throat and she clutched her sides as hysteria threatened to take over completely.

"What are you laughing at?" asked Blackfoot, his eyes mirthful. "Harold's in a lot of trouble."

"I—I know," Cole sputtered, "and poor Agnes might have really hurt herself." And laughter, inappropriately, came over her once more.

"I doubt it." Blackfoot had begun to chuckle by this time, too, though it seemed directed more at Cole than toward the earlier scenario. "Agnes probably wears good heavy army boots."

Cole would have collapsed again, but the unspent laughter died in her throat when the balloon suddenly caracoled downward, its trajectory viciously awry. Cole stiffened at first, then realized that Blackfoot was going to need another pair of steady hands and a clear head if they were going to get out of these rotors unscathed.

No sooner had she formed the thought than *Stargrazer* climbed drunkenly skyward. As though riding a mammoth roller coaster, they plummeted and soared, each descent lower and faster and infinitely more terrifying. The trees seemed to be rushing up to greet them and Cole thought surely they would soon score the tops of them; but then Blackfoot gave her the order to ballast and furiously they dumped sand until *Stargrazer* pulled herself up again, soaring wildly to the clouds, only to be yanked down once more by another rotor. Out went more sand, bag after bag, with alarming speed, until *Stargrazer* catapulted upward. Then the manic winds caught her again. Thus they continued for what seemed an eternity—up and down, lurching and soaring with no time to think or evaluate.

Blackfoot and Cole worked like cogs of the same machine, their minds and their bodies attuned to the crisis so that words became unnecessary. Cole drew strength from Blackfoot's nearness, which inspired her to move quickly and responsibly. Beyond the conscious limits of her mind, she sensed that Blackfoot, too, found her presence comforting.

In eerie silence, they bounced and whooshed as helplessly as a feather thrashing in the wind. "Hang in there," Blackfoot called out, expending a few precious seconds to ensure Cole's well-being. "I see the farm up ahead."

Cole glanced eastward and spied the tip of a cheery windmill beyond a heavy stand of trees. The rotors were lessening in intensity, but there was still too much to do to think about the landing.

"We can't let the dragrope down yet," Blackfoot said during a lull, his brow furrowed. "It might catch in the trees."

"That's all right," Cole replied, slightly breathless. "I've lived through a few vertical landings in my time." She clenched her teeth, omitting the fact that landings at the best of times terrified her. Her eyes clung to the approaching target as if she might somehow be able to will them there visually.

The trees were like rapidly approaching torpedoes as Blackfoot held the release valve open and *Stargrazer* fell. Mere seconds before grazing the tips of the conifers, the balloon leveled off and flew at a barely respectable height.

Cole heaved a sigh of relief. Blackfoot had been more meticulous than she thought; the lower they flew now, the easier the landing.

"All right, here we go," he uttered tersely when the clearing was imminent. "When I tell you to pull the rip line, pull! There's no room for a second try."

"Roger!" Cole's fingers curled around the red rope as if she was hanging on for her life.

They came to the edge of the trees and Blackfoot lowered the dragrope over the edge of the gondola, maneuvering it along the fallow ground like a rudder. By now, they were no more than a few feet in the air, sailing swiftly across the field. Blackfoot released more of the rope. Then just as the gondola touched ground, he called out, "Pull!" and Cole pulled the rip line.

Like a huge mythical bird shot in midflight, *Stargrazer* collapsed, her orb of indigo stretched out lifeless across the barren ground. Facing the direction of their flight, Cole and Blackfoot were braced low in the basket. One of Cole's hands gripped the gondola; the other was wrapped in Blackfoot's. Warm and dry as ever, she thought with amazement, acutely aware of her own stress-dampened body.

After coming to a final jouncing stop, they waited. The gondola remained upright in a picture-perfect landing. Blackfoot turned to Cole with his sparkling emerald gaze. "Nice work," he said softly. "We make a good team, you and I."

2

A FEW HOURS LATER Cole found herself wedged between stacks of Styrofoam coolers and dismantled tents in the rear of a bus full of scouts. She glanced down to assess the grass stains and the rust marks and the grease spots on her jump suit and wondered what had possessed her to wear white for a balloon race and jamboree.

But then, in all fairness, Warren's unexpected phone call had wakened her up from a deep sleep, and she'd never been one to function rationally on less than eight hours a night. In fact, if she'd been less groggy, she probably never would have agreed to undertake such a venture at the last minute.

Blackfoot was seated at the other end of the bus, his firmly muscled legs stretched out across the aisle. He had just finished leading the scouts through a lusty, albeit paraphrased, pirate ditty, and now, at the boys' unanimous insistence, he had launched into a haunting Indian legend. No one would have guessed by looking at him that he'd just completed a hundred-mile balloon race. Energy danced from Blackfoot's spirited eyes and the tones of his gruff, bristly voice were strong and full of vigor. All of the scouts seemed to know who he was and hung on his every word, as boys of that age do with their heroes. Even Cole soon found herself perched at the edge of her seat, entranced not only with the unfolding story but with the storyteller as well.

She wondered who he was, this Blackfoot. And where he came from. If he dabbled at all in the Philadelphia social scene, she'd have heard of him by now. A man like that was too compelling to blend into a crowd. If it weren't for his contemporary attire, he might easily have stepped from the pages of American folklore; he had a sort of pioneer ruggedness about him. Yet Cole sensed in him a subtle quality of sophistication . . . nothing so base as snobbery, but more the classic ease of a man who knows his own worth.

The old bus lurched and rattled and bounced them back to the launch site. All the while, Cole's curiosity grew, gnawing at her. She strained to hear bits of conversation between Blackfoot and the boys, anything that might give her a clue as to the identity of *Stargrazer*'s pilot. But she learned nothing beyond some facts about life on a reservation and the various qualities of reef knots and half hitches.

What was even worse than Cole's niggling curiosity was her growing concern that Blackfoot and *Stargrazer* might fly out of her life at the end of the day as quickly and silently as they'd entered it. And she couldn't imagine why that very real possibility worried her. She was just lately beginning to feel comfortable with her life and its little triumphs. The last thing in the world she needed now was to develop an obsession for some latter-day Lone Ranger.

Nevertheless, for a moment Cole actually entertained the idea of tapping one of the Boy Scouts on the shoulder and asking him what he knew about Blackfoot—the masked man, as it were. But then she decided it wasn't right to grill some poor, unsuspecting eleven-year-old. Besides, she'd just finished flying a five-hour race with the man; it was nobody's fault but her own if she couldn't get him to open up about himself. She would simply have to wait until she talked to Warren and drag it all out of him.

Cole tried to suppress the pull of disappointment when the bus turned into the parking lot of the launch site, though her sentiments clearly matched those of sixteen moaning and groaning scouts. The boys, in keeping with their chivalric training, assisted Cole out of the bus first. Blackfoot stayed inside to help unload the equipment. Soon the grounds were a flurry of frantic activity as troop leaders tried to find charges and issued instructions as to where tents would be set up.

In the midst of all the chaos, Cole spotted a scout who was much smaller than his peers struggling with the zipper of his camp bag. Cole went to him, knelt down and asked if she could be of any help.

"I used to have a duffel bag just like this one," she told the shy, freckled child, "and it always got stuck at the worst possible times."

"What did you do?" the boy asked, bravely sniffing back tears. Cole suspected he was suffering as much from homesickness as frustration with the zipper.

"Well, first I'd check to see if there were any threads caught in it and if not I'd grab hold of the bag real tight . . . like this. Then I'd take the zipper tab and hold it real tight, too . . . and pull just as hard as I could!" Cole pulled and the zipper opened, none the worse for wear.

The boy looked up with eyes full of gratitude. "Gee, thanks, ma'am."

Cole grinned. "You're welcome."

"That was nice of Ms Jameson to help you out like that, wasn't it, Tad?" The gruff, bristly voice came from behind.

"Sure was," Tad replied earnestly.

Cole turned around to find Blackfoot standing there. She must have looked up too quickly for suddenly she felt a little light-headed and had to touch her fingers to the ground before she could stand. On the other hand, it could have been merely the aftereffects of a long flight affecting her balance, she decided in retrospect.

Blackfoot's craggy face relaxed in a smile. "Walk you to your car?"

Cole felt her heart leap, exactly the way it had a lifetime ago when the boy next door had offered to carry her books to school. "Okay," she answered, in a voice that almost sounded young again. But of course that was nonsense. She wasn't young again. She was thirty-one, divorced and well past the stage of fluttering over a strange man who wasn't even her type.

She fell in with Blackfoot's stride and tried to remind herself that he was only walking her to her car. After all, he had an example to set for several thousand scouts.

"I had a wonderful time today," Cole said, after pointing out her small white sports car.

When they came to the car, Blackfoot leaned up against it and folded his arms. "Did you? Good, so did I. You're a fine balloonist."

Cole felt two uncharacteristic spots of crimson appear on her cheeks; she looked down and kicked a stone with her toe. Good grief, was she now going to respond with a fitting, "Aw, shucks"? All he'd done was comment on her ballooning aptitude, and for all she knew, he might have tossed the line off simply because they were now safe on the ground.

Finally, she managed to look up and utter, "Thanks. You're not so bad yourself...at ballooning, that is." The pause and the unnecessary clarification were enough to make the ensuing moment of silence that much more awkward.

Blackfoot, at least, was gracious enough not to comment. Instead, he lifted a large, square hand to his chin. "Are you doing anything tomorrow night?"

"Uh...not that I can think of," Cole replied, grinning in unconscious response to the nice ripple of excitement running through her. "But I don't think I'm up to another race."

Blackfoot laughed. The sound struck Cole as eminently satisfying, if all too rarely heard. "Me neither," he admitted. "I was thinking more along the lines of an awards dinner being held at the Franklin Institute. The mayor is the guest speaker."

So he wasn't going to fly right out of her life.

"It sounds like fun," said Cole. "Is that when we get to find out who won the race?"

"Yes." He swept open fingers through auburn curls. "Normally, Warren would have gone with me, but since you were the copilot..."

Something in Cole's expression must have made Blackfoot realize how he'd sounded, for his words trailed off and his eyes flickered with embarrassment. Immediately, Cole chided herself for being so sensitive. If her name had been Joe Green, he'd still be inviting her to the awards dinner; it was no big deal.

"I'd love to attend the dinner," she said at last, and before she could stop herself, added, "shall I have my tux cleaned?"

A smile of guilt and relief crept across Blackfoot's face. "Guess I had that one coming to me. Do you have something I can write your address on?"

"I can meet you there if you prefer," Cole suggested.

"No, that's okay. I'd like to pick you up." He paused, and his green eyes lingered on her a moment. "I guess if it had been Warren . . ."

"Don't tell me. You'd have picked him up, too," Cole said, laughing.

Blackfoot lifted his hands in a gesture of defeat. "No, I was going to say if it had been Warren standing here instead of me, he'd have carried it off a lot smoother than I have."

Cole smiled and lowered her eyes to dig out a business card from her wallet. He was right, she thought as she printed her address on the back. Warren Sanders would have handled this situation with his usual flawless panache. But if it had been Warren asking, she wouldn't be looking forward to the evening with nearly as much pleasure as she was right now. Cole handed Blackfoot her card. "What time shall I expect you?"

Blackfoot's fists were shoved into the front pockets of his khaki slacks. He looked as though he couldn't quite believe she'd accepted his invitation.

Goodness, he was adorable when he looked unsure of himself, Cole thought absurdly. She couldn't tell whether it was shyness on her part or caution. Whatever it was, it was not an unappealing quality in a man. A far cry from the flashy, gregarious types she dealt with in advertising every day.

"Is seven okay?" Blackfoot asked.

"Seven's fine. See you then." Cole opened the car door and stepped inside. As she drove through the exit gates of the parking lot, she could see Blackfoot through her rearview mirror. When he lifted his hand to her in one final wave, Cole couldn't help but smile.

TWO BAGS OF GROCERIES and a parcel held in place with her chin made it impossible for Cole to knock on Warren's door, so she used her knee to announce her arrival.

"Come in. It's open," Warren's voice called out from the other side in response to her muffled pounding.

Cole hiked one bag onto her hip, muttered something about coming in being easier said than done, then twisted the doorknob with two fingers and pushed it open an instant before the parcel slipped off the top of the bag and fell into the entryway. "Oh, for Pete's sake."

"Good morning, gorgeous." Warren Sanders, tall, blond and handsome, looked oddly vulnerable lying flat on his back in the middle of the living-room floor. He was propped at head and knees by cushions and covered with an afghan, crafted, no doubt, by one of his many erstwhile female companions.

"Hi, there! My, do you ever look cozy," Cole replied cheerily as she bent to recover the parcel and place it on a chair. With the two bags of groceries, she crossed the room, passing high-tech chrome-and-cushion furniture and neon sculptures inspired by the *Kama Sutra*. Cole deposited the bags on the kitchen counter and turned to study her best friend.

Warren was the personification of nearly every woman's fantasy of the perfect male. He could have made a fortune with his face and body as one of those impossibly virile men who persuade people to buy cologne merely on the basis of photogenic sex appeal. But Warren was too clever to depend on the vagaries of fashion. It was his quick mind that had earned him a fortune as the golden boy of the advertising world. Charming, polished and seductively aggressive, he was easily one of Philadelphia's most eligible bachelors. And if that weren't already enough, he'd been in love with Cole for years.

"How are you feeling this morning?" Cole asked him. "Any better?"

Warren shook his head carefully. "Not much. I tried crawling to the cereal cupboard this morning and covered about four inches. The doctor says it's a pretty bad muscle tear."

Cole drew her brows together in a look of concern. "You poor fellow. I should have gotten here earlier. You must be ravenous."

"The sight of you always makes me ravenous, sweetheart," Warren countered, his blue eyes glinting devilishly.

"Warren," said Cole, smiling, "you're full of it."

The two of them had known each other for years, ever since Cole started at the advertising agency as a receptionist. She was long accustomed to Warren's effusive banter and was one of the few people who knew he wasn't a phony, unlike so many in the business who were. He genuinely loved being with people, women especially, and couldn't help exhibiting his love constantly.

As for his oft-mentioned feelings toward her, Cole suffered no delusions. Oh, she knew that Warren genuinely believed himself in love with her, but she also knew herself to be one of the very few women in his life who hadn't succumbed to his charms. It was the classic tale of what a person can't have, a person wants.

When Cole first met Warren, she was married. Later, when she became separated from her husband, she was too hurt and too vulnerable to dare seek comfort in Warren's eager arms. After the divorce, in spite of Warren's many attributes, Cole simply didn't hear bells when she was with him. She could never spend her life with a man who considered everything a game, a conquest, a battle of wits. He was matchless as a friend, but as a lover? Never.

She suspected Warren understood the situation as well as she did. Undoubtedly, it was their mutual respect for each other's feelings that kept the friendship strong. She knew Warren would never back her into a corner about the nature of their platonic relationship, nor would Cole ever wound his ego by stating her case aloud.

"So what do you have in the bags?" Warren asked eagerly.

Cole shrugged. "Not much. Just a few of your deli favorites. Corned beef, kaisers, those big fat garlic dills, potato salad . . ." She deliberately trailed off.

Warren's eyes glistened. "And?"

"What do you mean, 'and'? You ought to be grateful!" Cole gave a lively toss of her black hair as she began to unload the bags.

"No dessert?"

"If you think I would waste my money on your very favorite—and highly overpriced—cherry cheesecake . . ."

He knew from her expression she was teasing. "You did remember! You're an angel, Cole. I love you!"

Cole turned her head away slightly, intent on unwrapping sliced meat. "I know, Warren," she said. "It's mutual."

At times, Cole wondered why she was being so hard on herself and Warren. At her age, she should have been willing to accept the fact that nothing was perfect, that the earth did not have to move for two people to be right for each other. In some ways, it would be the easiest thing in the world for her to share her life with Warren. She wouldn't have to sacrifice much. There were no children from previous marriages to consider; he'd never married. She wouldn't have to move to a new city or quit her job. They would become known as one of the city's perfect couples with a membership in the finest country club, exotic vacations, perhaps even their own advertising firm someday. For goodness' sake, what more could a woman ask for? Yet, no matter how often she asked herself the question, the same objection kept cropping up. She didn't love him.

"What'd you think of Blackfoot?" Warren asked, right out of the blue.

Cole had just gotten cutlery from the drawer when he asked the question. She jerked up suddenly and the silverware spilled onto the counter with a clatter. Given the circumstances, it was a perfectly reasonable question; there was no call to become defensive.

"Uh, I...he's an interesting sort of fellow." Cole looked up and pinned a vaguely disinterested smile on her face. "He's a little peculiar, maybe. You said you knew him from college, didn't you?"

"Yeah, we were in the same dorm, but he was a couple of years ahead of me."

Grateful for the diversion of arranging pickles on a dish, Cole asked, "How well do you know him?"

"Not that well. Blackfoot's never been much of a socializer."

"Oh." Cole placed two thick corned-beef sandwiches on a plate, put the plate on a tray and carried it all into the living room. "What's Blackfoot's real name?"

Warren's face was inextricably drawn to the sight of his favorite foods. He took the plate of sandwiches from Cole, placed it on his chest and launched into the first one, savoring the corned beef with maddening deliberateness before answering. "Why? Didn't he tell you who he was?"

"No, he didn't," Cole replied, oddly irritated. "He said he doesn't use his real name much, and he doesn't even work. Getting that man to talk was like pulling teeth. And to be stuck in a balloon with him for five hours..."

Laughing, Warren said, "He does take some getting used to, but I assure you there's nothing weird about the guy. He's just a bit of a loner." Warren polished off the rest of his sandwich before resting his head on the cushion, fatigued by the exertion. "Blackfoot doesn't work because he has enough money to live off the interest on his interest for the rest of his life."

"You're kidding," Cole said, astonished. Nothing about Blackfoot, apart from *Stargrazer*, had alluded to his wealth. "So who is he?"

"His name is Adam Torrie."

Cole thought a moment, then her eyes widened. "You mean the Torries of Rittenhouse Square? The rubber magnates?"

"One and the same."

"I didn't think there were any Torries left. Their home is a museum now, isn't it?"

"Yeah, but Blackfoot doesn't spend much time in Philadelphia. As far as I know, he is the only surviving descendant."

Cole took a pickle and crunched into it, chewing thoughtfully. "So where does he spend his time?"

"Before I answer your question, would you mind handing me that slice of cheesecake, please? I promise to eat my other sandwich afterward."

Cole grimaced but did as she was asked.

"Let me see," said Warren. "Where does Blackfoot spend his time? Offhand, I can think of Kathmandu...the Serengeti...Papua New Guinea, the New Hebrides..."

"Is he still involved with the rubber business?"

Warren shook his head. "If I remember correctly, the Torries got out of rubber in his grandfather's day. Blackfoot's father went into medicine."

"So I understand. Then why does Blackfoot travel so much?"

"Because he likes it, I suppose."

Cole got up to fill the kettle for instant coffee, the only kind Warren stocked. "People don't travel all the time just to travel," she muttered with a derisive sniff.

"Why not, if they can afford it?"

"Well . . . because it's . . . oh, I don't know. You know how I am; it just seems so nonproductive." She spooned Nescafé into two mugs. "Funny thing is, Blackfoot didn't strike me as the jet-setter type."

"I never said he was."

"Sure you did. You said he does nothing but live off the family fortune."

"No, you asked me where Blackfoot spends his time, not how he spends it. From what I can gather, he shows up every few years to drum up money for starving kids, then disappears again. He probably does it for the tax write-off."

"Warren, you make him sound so callous."

Her friend shrugged. "I'm just telling you what I know. Besides, I just balloon with the guy. I don't ask for credentials."

Cole shook her head as she filled the mugs with boiling water. "Honestly, men form the strangest alliances. . . . Oh, I almost forgot. I brought something for you." She brought the coffees to Warren's space on the floor then went to retrieve the parcel near the door.

Warren took the package wrapped in brown paper and smiled. "Do you buy your get-well gifts in advance too?"

She cast him a droll look. "No, smarty, I do not buy get-well gifts in advance! Only birthday and Christmas gifts, and cards and gift-wrap. You could save yourself a bundle, Warren, if you did all your shopping in January."

"No doubt," he admitted as he unwrapped the package. "But I never know who I'm going to meet during the year, do I?"

Cole grudgingly acknowledged he had a point.

"Hey, Cole, these are great!" he exclaimed when he saw the stack of video cassettes. "Burt Reynolds, Clint Eastwood...even the classic Steve McQueens." He gave her a dazzling look of gratitude. "You would not believe what it's like watching children's educational programming, although I now know how to make egg-carton caterpillars."

Cole replied with a laugh. "If you're still not up and around by the time you finish these, I can take them back and get some new ones. They're yours for a week."

"I'm so starved for entertainment, I'll probably be through them by tonight."

"Sorry," Cole blurted. "Can't get any for you tonight. I'm going to the awards dinner with—" For some reason, she hadn't intended to tell Warren about her plans, and now that they'd slipped out, she felt unaccountably sheepish.

"You're attending the awards dinner with Blackfoot, you were going to say?"

"Well . . . sure, why not?" breezed Cole. "I figure I'm entitled to some compensation for spending all that time with your strange friend."

Warren rubbed his eyes with fatigue. "It must be these painkillers that are fogging my brain. You've got the hots for the guy, haven't you?"

"Oh, Warren, please! What a barbaric expression. And it's not true at all." Cole, with marked indignation, began to gather up the remains of Warren's lunch.

"Listen to me, Cole. I'm not telling you this just 'cause I've been left on the sidelines. You know that cliché about rolling stones? It could have been inspired by Blackfoot."

Cole tossed an over-the-shoulder look on her way to the kitchen. "And I suppose you're going to say the part about the moss refers to me?"

"If the shoe fits, sweetheart. . . I'm just trying to save you a lot of grief. If it's a home and kids you want, he's not the guy for you."

"Home and kids?" Cole slapped her hand to her chest. "Me? Don't be preposterous, Warren!" Abruptly, emphatically, she changed the subject.

WARREN WAITED until he heard Cole's car drive away and, for good measure, allowed an extra couple of minutes before lifting the afghan off his knees and getting up. Good thing she'd left when she did, or this back injury of his might have turned out to be legitimate. Hardwood floors were a far cry from a king-size water bed.

He stood up and stretched his arms high above his tautly muscled frame. Funny, he was feeling better about this than he thought he would. The sensation of being kicked in the stomach wasn't nearly as painful as the first time he realized he'd never have Cole Jameson for himself. That had to be a good sign. Sure, maybe he'd laid on the reverse psychology a little thick this morning, the white lies a shade too gray, but all in all, things had worked out not too badly.

Cole was intrigued, that much was certain, and Blackfoot had done precisely what Warren hoped he would by asking Cole to the awards dinner. He knew both of them well enough to know they'd both turn out looking like a million bucks for the event. After that, well, it was just a matter of letting the old black magic take its course.

Crossing the room to the fridge, Warren opened the door and brought out a beer. He still wouldn't put it past his old buddy to do something idiotic like shake Cole's hand at the end of the evening and take the next flight to anywhere, but maybe he really would find her impossible to resist. After all, even though some habits were tough to break, Blackfoot had been on his own a hell of a long time, almost too long. Unfortunately, that could prove to be the biggest hitch, and there was no way Warren would be able to step in anymore and help things along. If either of them were to entertain even the slightest suspicion . . .

In a rare expression of sentimentality, Warren held the dark brown bottle aloft in a solitary toast. "To Cole and Blackfoot, I love you both, so . . . go for it."

3

COLE STOOD ankle deep in discarded choices of attire from her closet. Everything she tried on was either too severe, too demure or too...something! Blackfoot had managed to escape yesterday without telling her what the dress requirements were. As she'd never attended a balloon fete before, she had no idea whether people went in khaki or crepe.

Not that it really mattered, she told herself as she splashed on a light after-shower cologne. This was not an occasion for long, hot bubble baths and Chanel, nor was there any justification for the butterflies that were executing aeronautical maneuvers in her stomach. It was only an awards dinner, and she was a mere replacement. Period.

Nevertheless, the prospect of an evening with Blackfoot reminded Cole of the second time she climbed aboard a hot-air balloon. The first time she had been excited and exhilarated by the sheer novelty of it. The second time, however, she had been sufficiently informed to be terrified.

There were so many unknown and contradictory elements to the man. Unlike most men she had known—including her ex-husband and Warren—Blackfoot could not be analyzed and classified into a neat, predictable little pigeonhole, and that inescapable fact unnerved her. She kept telling herself it was only a matter of enduring a few hours with him—no reason to view it with the trauma of one's very first date.

Finally, through the process of elimination, Cole decided on a shimmering satin evening suit in a deep ruby red, guaranteed to outshine butterflies. Its straight lines set off the shoulder-length blunt cut of her hair and the ivory smoothness of her skin and made her appear sleek, elegant and utterly composed.

The bedroom clock told Cole she still had enough time to pick up the other scattered garments and return them to hangers before they were indelibly wrinkled. As she tidied up, she silently remonstrated herself for the shabby and uncharacteristic way she had handled her wardrobe.

Downstairs, Cole tossed the jacket of her suit over a chair and sat down to wait. Five minutes passed...ten. Blackfoot was late. The colossal nerve of the man! Cole stood up and began to pace while the clock tauntingly ticked away the minutes.

At twenty minutes past seven, by which time much of Cole's resilience had wilted, the door bell finally rang. She opened the door, more than ready to serve Blackfoot with a well-rehearsed diatribe. But when she saw him, she forgot everything she'd wanted to say.

Blackfoot, in a white shirt and three-piece dark-blue suit, was the quintessential Philadelphia gentleman. His curls shone, slightly damp, and his face held a warm and tawny sheen. He looked...devastating. "Sorry I'm late," he said, his green eyes taking control over Cole's wide-open blue ones. "I was reading a...an article, and I lost track of the time."

"That's all right," Cole insisted, though inwardly aghast to hear herself pronounce instant remission. Reading an article? What kind of an excuse was that? Any other man would have had the decency to come up with a lie!

As Blackfoot stepped inside, Cole caught the faint masculine essence of him—clean, tangy and somehow bristly, like his voice and the stubborn shadow of whiskers that still framed his freshly shaven face. The sensation inspired a strange tickle behind Cole's breastbone that merely intensified when she tried to take a deep breath.

Blackfoot was taking his time to admire her. Eyes half closed, he lingered on her face, then circled the frame of straight black hair that brushed her bare shoulders. He lowered brown lashes to study the hollow at the base of her throat and descended even further to the décolletage above her ruby camisole.

Cole felt her skin flush to a deep shade of apricot. She had never known anyone with eyes so penetrating, so unapologetically bold. She should have been incensed, or at the very least made some vague gesture to distract him, but her body seemed to be reacting with a will of its own, drawn to the source of admiration like a moth to a flame.

"You look stunning," said Blackfoot in his gruff voice, a barely perceptible smile lifting his lips.

"Th-thank you," Cole said, and brought her hand to her throat. "Would you . . . uh, care for a drink before we go?" It sounded like there was a fly buzzing around in her throat, which she discreetly tried to evict.

"No, thanks. We should be on our way. But first, I have something for you." Blackfoot held out a small box Cole hadn't noticed earlier.

She opened it and found an exquisite, perfectly formed white orchid devoid of any adornment beyond its own dazzling fragility. Cole couldn't remember the last time a man had given her a corsage. Prom night? The managerial women and liberated men who lived in the fast lane routinely scoffed at such tokens, but Cole couldn't help but be delighted.

"You look like a person who should wear orchids," Blackfoot said, as if in quiet defence of the gesture.

When Cole looked up, the room had misted. "It's beautiful, Blackfoot. Will you help me pin it on?"

For some reason, she had expected him to be clumsy, but she was wrong. This wasn't high-school prom night, after all, and Blackfoot was no awkward teenager. His strong brown fingers handled the delicate bloom with a gossamer touch, pinning it above her left breast. She was acutely aware of the gentle grazing of his fingers against her chest and the whisper of his breath on her skin as he bent to fasten the pin. No less captivating were the simple nearness of his body, the sound of his deep and regular breathing, the weathered ruggedness of his neck and the brown curls that coiled evenly around his head. Cole didn't even realize she was holding her breath until Blackfoot stepped back and she felt slightly faint.

"Perfect," he declared in typical, terse summation. He ushered Cole outside to an expensive black sports car awaiting them at the curb. He let her in and walked around to the driver's side while Cole perused her surroundings. The car was low-slung and streamlined, almost decadent in its rich leathery luxury.

Cole, practically reclining in the seat, noticed with chagrin that the slit of her narrow ruby skirt was wide open and revealing much more thigh than she would have liked. But she had worn this skirt plenty of times without worrying overly much about its seductive elements. If she was so uncertain of her ability to carry it off, it might have been better to go with navy and a Peter Pan collar, she told herself brusquely, tugging at the slippery fabric. It didn't mean she was trying to snare the man or anything!

"Leave it," Blackfoot admonished, much to her surprise, when he slid into his side of the car. His eyes glinted like emeralds, the fiery facets igniting the length of Cole's legs as her hands dropped helplessly into her lap. "That's what the slit is there for, isn't it?" he asked, without a trace of rancor.

Cole's jaw dropped and her cheeks blazed at the outright audacity of his comment. "Why, you—" Oh, the hell with it, she thought, and turned to stare sightlessly at the row of red-brick, white-shuttered condominiums on her street. At times like this, denial was as good as admission. Mercifully, Blackfoot did not pursue the topic, so Cole ignored the skirt.

He expertly maneuvered the car through the narrow streets, while Cole surreptitiously allowed herself a visual assessment of him, based on the newly acquired information from Warren. Even in the lateral angles of the low-slung car, Blackfoot's suit fit well. An expensive Italian cut, it revealed the precise amount of French silk cuff at the sleeve, and the expertly tailored slacks rode easily above his ankle as he depressed the accelerator. The black shoes were sharkskin—custom-made, no doubt. Cole had to give him credit. When he put his mind to it, the man wore his legacy with consummate ease.

By the time they arrived at the Franklin Institute, the reception was well under way, the room full of a colorful assortment of flying enthusiasts. Cole and Blackfoot worked their way slowly through the crowd, many of whom Cole knew from her flying club.

She lifted a glass of champagne from a passing tray and was distinctly aware of people studying her escort with candid curiosity. So she wasn't the only one who felt the impact of his presence, she thought with a certain glimmer of satisfaction.

Blackfoot mingled easily, garnering anecdotes and tales with little apparent effort. It was an observation that surprised Cole. She had always prided herself on being able to make people relax in a relatively short space of time, but hers was nothing compared to Blackfoot's ability. He was drawing people out of themselves and acting as though he held a vital interest in even the most mundane of their small talk. But then, come to think of it, she'd done her share of babbling with him the day before. Something about him seemed to inspire confidence.

Cole wondered whether it was evident to anyone else or if it was simply her imagination, but it seemed that Blackfoot, despite his convivial melding, kept himself detached. Part of the crowd, yet not part of it. Something in the studied lines between his brows suggested a mere tolerance bordering on impatience. Cole couldn't help but think that given the choice, Blackfoot would sooner be flying five thousand feet above this gala than be here in the midst of it.

When a moment finally came when the two of them were alone and not part of any other conversation, Cole took the opportunity to move closer to him. "I didn't get a chance to commend you properly on your piloting abilities yesterday," she said with a smile.

Blackfoot's face eased into an expression of amusement. "I assumed the look of gratitude you gave me when we landed was meant to convey that message."

Cole laughed. "Let me assure you, it was. At the time, I thought you were unbelievably reckless, the way you handled those rotors. But looking back on it, I think you knew exactly what you were doing."

Blackfoot shook his head and took a slow sip of neat whiskey. "No one ever knows precisely what he's doing in a balloon. But therein lies the excitement, right?"

Cole wondered what it was about the way he said that that made her heart suddenly quiver like a bow.

"Just out of curiosity," Blackfoot said, "how would you have handled those rotors?"

"I'd have flown the race higher. We'd have been safer in the long run, and probably would have landed somewhere in New Jersey."

Blackfoot responded with a rich, deep laugh. "Nothing wrong with that approach, as long as winning the race isn't important." He put down his half-full glass. "I must admit, though, there is an element of risk in flying by one's instincts and attempting to use inclement elements to one's advantage. All a person needs is the interference of one negative emotion—anger or fear, for example—and it can be enough to plow you into the side of a mountain."

Cole shuddered. "I never thought of it that way before. Is that why you were so reluctant to fly with me . . . in case I inspired some negative emotion?"

"That was part of the reason," Blackfoot conceded, his jaw set in the position of someone who had just admitted half of the whole truth and had no intention of revealing the rest.

Tiring suddenly of waiting for clarifications that never came, Cole decided to try a more direct approach. "Warren told me who you really are."

Blackfoot raised one eyebrow. "Oh? I wasn't aware that I'd been deceiving you."

"Well, no," Cole said, shifting her weight from one foot to another, "you didn't exactly deceive me, but I got the distinct impression that you don't care to be known by your family name. I mean, it's not as though the Torries were pirates or anything."

"On the contrary. They were philanthropic to a fault."

Their eyes met and Cole waited. He was going to do it again, leave her hanging. . . .

"Perhaps I should explain," he said, astonishing Cole as much as if he'd begun to speak in Greek. "The Torries, you see, made their fortune in rubber at the turn of the century. But it was the pursuit of that fortune that killed my grandmother and two of my uncles—not to mention hundreds of plantation workers who couldn't tolerate fourteen-hour days and backbreaking labor."

"I'm sorry," Cole said, regretting her ill-placed curiosity. Of course, that was probably why Blackfoot was telling her this—to teach her a lesson.

He pressed on. "My grandmother insisted on accompanying her husband to Ghana, where the largest plantations were. She also brought their three sons, because she couldn't bear the idea of their growing up in Philadelphia, never knowing their father. Malaria killed her within the year, as well as my uncles, who were six and four at the time. Only my father, an infant, survived."

Cole felt the pain of Blackfoot's story twist through her heart like a knife. "How tragic for them. Is that why your grandfather sold the business?"

"Yes, he came back to Philadelphia, gave my father over to be raised by nannies and drank himself to death."

"I can understand how you must feel," she said softly.

Blackfoot's face hardened. "No, you don't, Cole. Nobody can." Then he turned and struck up a conversation with somebody else, as though they'd just finished chatting about the weather.

Dinner was a boisterous affair and Cole might have enjoyed herself if she had been there with Warren, or anyone other than that enigma of a man named Blackfoot. She was seated across from him at a long, crowded table; conversation was nearly impossible. The man next to her was suffering an overindulgence of martinis, and his breath made Cole reel every time he slurred something in her direction. On the other side of her was a woman, but Cole never saw anything but the back of her head. Blackfoot, as the meal wore on, had become less communicative with those seated beside him, though his eyes wandered frequently in Cole's direction. She couldn't tell why he kept looking at her—the gaze seemed out of place for an occasion such as this. It was with acute relief that Cole saw the awards were about to be presented.

The toastmaster introduced Philadelphia's handsome young mayor, who stood up to warm applause and made a few well-chosen remarks about ballooning. Philadelphia's first citizen, Benjamin Franklin, had been an avid proponent of the fledgling sport and the city had been the site of America's first manned balloon flight, in 1793.

"So it gives me great pleasure, ladies and gentlemen," said the mayor, "to announce the winners of yesterday's competition, who will go on to represent Philadelphia at the prestigious Jean Beauvais Race of the World's Greatest Cities, to be held later this year in France."

A thrill of anticipatory pleasure washed over Cole, followed just as swiftly by the deflating realization that she wasn't a part of *Stargrazer*'s flight crew. She had merely been filling in.

"The winning balloon," the mayor went on to say, "which landed a scant eight inches off target, was *Stargrazer*—" A burst of applause threatened to drown out the rest of his announcement, but Cole still managed to hear "—piloted by Dr. Adam Torrie, or Blackfoot, as he is called by those of us who know him. *Stargrazer*'s copilot was Ms Nicole Jameson."

Doctor? Those of us who know him? It was amid such irrelevant reflections that Cole was nudged out of her seat by well-wishers. She stood up and watched, as if in slow motion, while Blackfoot came around the table, linked her arm around his, and took her to the podium to accept the award.

Cole's eyes skimmed over the crowd as Blackfoot spoke a few words of thanks. Then her gaze slid to his profile and she saw the strength in his jaw; she saw in his eyes a spirit shot through with such integrity as to be almost intimidating; and she saw gentleness in his mouth. He would be the perfect envoy for Philadelphia, the archetypal adventurer, the stuff of legendary heroes like those who had built the country. It was suddenly inexplicably tearing her apart that she would not be at Blackfoot's side when he accepted the even greater award in France.

When the speeches were finished, the reception began to disintegrate into a noisy maelstrom.

"Let's get out of here," said Blackfoot, taking Cole's arm and leading her through the crowd, his trophy tucked under one arm.

Cole had no intention of arguing. The cool night air revived her like a splash of water, though it did little to soothe her enflamed thoughts. What had started out as a simple favor for a friend was now beginning to take over the last vestiges of her well-ordered life.

She would have been the last to believe a man like Blackfoot could drop into her life and turn it upside down. The scion of an old family, a doctor—though of what she had no idea—and friend of the mayor, no less. Not that any of those things mattered to her; she was no status seeker. Cole was more impressed by Blackfoot's prowess as an aeronaut and by his ability to charm everybody from scouts to politicians. Admittedly, she was not unmoved by his physical attributes, either: his quiet, solid strength, his remarkable green eyes . . . his laugh.

Cole knew now she wanted to see more of him, but considering her thoroughly botched attempt at conversation this evening, it seemed unlikely. Besides, even if she did see him again, what would it accomplish and where would it lead? Not much and nowhere, came the curt replies from her conscience. Warren had been right when he'd warned of the impracticalities of a match between Cole, the plodder and Blackfoot, the enigmatic wanderer.

Blackfoot parked his car in front of Cole's condominium and escorted her up the short flight of steps to her front door. She turned her head slightly, using the light of the street lamp to riffle through her purse for her key. A sheath of black hair slid across Cole's face, hiding her features while she worked out her predicament.

This was not the Cole Jameson whom everybody knew as extroverted and eternally in charge of her situation. A few knew how sensitive and unsure she was underneath, but since her divorce Cole had cultivated an outer reserve that kept unwelcome intruders at arm's length. Cole had learned how to lift an eyebrow a certain way to discourage a pass from an exuberant male client. She knew how to hand a man a drink with the unspoken message that it was to be his last. In four scary years of independence, the tried and true methods had never failed.

In this case, however, the tried and true methods hardly seemed appropriate. For one thing, she wasn't certain of what she wanted or dared to expect from Blackfoot. All she knew was that she didn't want the evening to end quite yet.

Lifting her head, Cole was about to form an invitation to come inside when she was taken captive by Blackfoot's eyes. His hand grazed the satin sleeve of her jacket and, with a slight pressure from his fingers, Blackfoot brought her around to face him squarely. His gaze raked over her upturned face; his hands gripped her shoulders, digging into her flesh without apology. Then the distance between them narrowed as he pulled her to him, blacking out the world with his kiss.

Cole swayed at the sudden, riveting contact of his hard body against her, at the raw conquest of her mouth. Briefly, her mind flickered with the memory of some dim and distant warning, but it soon melted beneath the blazing reality of the present.

Subconsciously, Cole had assumed Blackfoot would be awkward and ungainly in the ways of pleasing a woman. But she'd been wrong—oh, so wrong—she realized now as her arms went up to clasp his neck.

His kiss was ravenous and his lips savored hers with such fervor that failure to respond was impossible. Angling his head deliberately, Blackfoot moved his tongue along Cole's mouth in a restless quest for fulfillment. When her lips parted, she felt the vibrations of a groan issued deep within Blackfoot's throat and then his tongue delved into her mouth.

She drew him in fully, blanking her mind to all but the rushing delirium of the moment. Intoxicated by the taste of him, her senses were heightened by the wisps of his breath against her cheek and by the rising pull of her body as it arched to meet his.

Blackfoot's thick auburn-tipped curls wrapped themselves around Cole's fingers, each one bestowing a sensuous miniature caress. She could feel his pulse racing beneath the sinews of his neck . . . or perhaps it was her own.

He took his time discovering the sweet contours of her mouth, darting and teasing, lingering and thrusting, each move subtly creating its own level of stimulation. Cole shifted her body ever so slightly and with a searing jolt her thigh came into contact with his fiery arousal. Instantly, everything inside her seemed to turn to water and Cole was certain she'd have fallen had Blackfoot's arms not been locked effectively around her waist.

His hand came up behind her head and his fingers entwined in her glossy black hair. With his other hand, Blackfoot sought the curve of her derriere and pressed her to him. With a whimper, Cole felt herself grind against him with unrestrained passion. Her body was in turmoil, a frightening, exhilarating sensation, every nerve and every fiber screaming for release.

But this was sheer madness, some distant echo cried. Who was supposed to be in control here? Cole felt as if she'd been tossed into an endless, whirling vortex, spinning and spinning helplessly out of control. Her only means of escape if she didn't stop now was the act of culmination. And that was out of the question. They were strangers to each other, their lives played on entirely different planes. One simply did not surrender on the spot, no matter how sweet the release promised to be.

Bit by agonizing bit, Cole gathered together the remnants of her composure, lifting her arms from his neck, pulling her mouth from his, stepping back against the door with jellied legs. Blackfoot, to her chagrin, was totally compliant. He released his hold on her at the first indication of resistance. He looked down at her with dark, rapacious eyes, and Cole was somewhat mollified to learn his desire had obviously been as staggering as her own.

"Would you like to come in for . . . coffee?" she asked weakly, the innocent and well-meant words betraying her rattled state.

The night air was splintered with sexual tension. The deserted streets mocked their untimely intimacy. Blackfoot seemed to be devouring her with his eyes, and Cole longed for the relative security of her living room where she might conceivably assume a role of hostess with some success, if nothing else.

"No, thanks," Blackfoot mumbled, backing down the stairs. "I have an early flight to catch tomorrow, and I still have to pack."

"Flight?" Cole echoed, desperately willing herself not to ask too much.

"Yes, I'm going to Switzerland, but thank you, Cole, for an . . . unforgettable weekend." Blackfoot turned quickly and descended the last two steps at once.

Cole watched as he climbed into his car and pulled away without so much as a backward glance. Then she looked down.

Her orchid was crushed.

4

ADAM KNEW the pretty blond flight attendant was hovering even before he lifted one reluctant eyelid and removed all doubt. Her perfume, whatever it was, smelled expensive, predatory and as subtle as an armored tank.

"Would you care for a drink, sir? Our bar is now open," she said in a softly guttural Swiss accent.

He had already refused a headset, reading material and a pillow; each time his eyes had been firmly closed. Why couldn't airlines supply Do Not Disturb signs for passengers to hang around their necks?

"What I'd really like," he told her with measured calm, "is some sleep. No meals, no drinks, maybe just some coffee before we land."

"Very well, sir," she chirped with a brisk, efficient smile. "Enjoy your flight."

Adam watched absently as the woman moved up the aisle in search of a more personable passenger. Satisfying himself that she'd connected with an eager, lusty-eyed businessman, he pushed his seat back even farther and shut his eyes.

After ten fruitless minutes of keeping them shut by force, Adam was ready to give up the battle. Maybe he would be better off passing the time by eating dinner, watching the movie and engaging in an innocuous business discussion with one of the many gray-suited, bored executives seated around him. Anything was better than lying here in this ridiculous saucer position and thinking about the past weekend.

He wasn't sure whether he ought to thank Warren Sanders or throttle him for his last-minute replacement. In his present frame of mind, he was leaning toward the latter. Not that it was Warren's fault that his back went out, but he could have sent a potbellied copilot named Harry or Bill. Balloon races were challenging enough without being distracted by the likes of Cole Jameson.

Come to think of it, Warren had to be going soft in the head to let a woman like her out of his sight. Granted, it had been a long time since Adam Torrie had been with a woman, but he still recognized class when he saw it. And Cole Jameson had plenty of class.

Adam closed his eyes—without trying this time— and discovered he could conjure up her image without the slightest effort. He had heard her voice first, challenging, softly defiant, with a surprisingly low timbre for a woman. When he turned around, he'd expected to find a woman his age with sultry, world-weary looks. What he did find was a woman who could have been twenty or forty or anywhere in between. Her voice was seductively deceptive.

First, there were those eyes of hers, huge and clear and so blue you could see forever in them, framed by lashes too thick and black to be believed. They were childlike eyes, open and trusting, but there was maturity in them, too. Perhaps it was in the pale violet shadows beneath them, or in the barely perceptible laugh lines at the corners.

The color of her hair was just as incredible, but on the morning of the race she had had it pulled back so tightly she might have been a schoolmarm from another century. Except that strands of it kept coming loose around her face, which drove her crazy. And no schoolmarm would have worn a white jump suit like that one and done it such justice. Cole was very definitely of this century.

She was a hard woman to figure out, when it came right down to it. She wasn't very tall, but she carried herself like someone with height who was proud of it. Shoulders back, chin high, she was the epitome of untouchable feminine confidence. Despite the fact that she was one of those glitzy advertising types, there was something about her that made him want to fight all her battles for her. Not only did he lack the time and the inclination to be anyone's Sir Galahad, but she'd probably belt him for the mere suggestion. A woman who called herself Cole and flew hot-air balloons for fun did not expect to be treated like a piece of bone china.

Adam silently chided himself. Whether Cole Jameson was a total pushover or tough as nails made no difference to him. If he did need a woman right now—and he wasn't denying the fact, by any means—she was going to have to be a woman who didn't need to be analyzed before you could touch her. The kind of woman who was content to see her man whenever he was in town, and willing to let him go the next morning with a kiss and a smile. Somehow, Cole didn't strike him as that type, which was too bad.

Damn! This was no good. Adam readjusted his seat and rubbed the back of his neck. If he didn't get some rest soon, he'd be no good to anybody in Geneva, and he couldn't afford to mess things up. There were too many people counting on him, and he'd worked too hard to let things fall apart now. Maybe if he just concentrated hard on nothing at all, put everything out of his mind . . .

So much for that idea. Just when it seemed he had succeeded, one irrepressible tentacle of Adam's mind would grope out and curl itself around the memory of Cole in a wine-colored dress, cut down to there and slit up to there. How in the name of heaven was a man supposed to concentrate on antiseptic white halls when there were warm, round curves in his not-too-distant past? It had been one dynamite dress with a body to match, and it had been all he could do to keep from staring all through the awards dinner, like some recently removed jungle primitive.

Of course, if he were completely honest with himself, he'd have to admit it wasn't only the dress that made him stare. It was that cool, delicately sculptured face of Cole's that revealed so little of her inner thoughts. And since when had he given a damn about what anybody thought? But like it or not, he'd sat through that interminable meal wondering whether she was bored or laughing on the inside or what.

What he wouldn't give to find out what ticked under that classy, professional veneer. If he'd had the time, he'd have taken her away somewhere, someplace private with plenty of atmosphere, and peeled away all the sexy, protective layers until there was nothing but the real Cole Jameson lying in his arms. Then he'd touch her all over, taste her, melt down every lingering fiber of her resistance until she was completely his—

"Oh, for God's sake!" Adam muttered aloud, jerking up in his seat and startling the gray-suited business traveler beside him.

"There is something wrong?" the man asked in a thick Italian accent.

Adam lifted one corner of his mouth in a sardonic grin. "Nothing that a double Scotch won't cure."

The man's face lit up with understanding. "Ah, it is a woman, no?"

"Yeah, I guess you could say that, but I'll get over it." Adam summoned the flight attendant, who was more than eager to finally be of some service.

The drink really didn't help much, but Adam forced it back anyway while his traveling companion regaled him with his own female woes. Adam stretched his legs out and smiled contentedly. In a couple of hours, he'd be in Switzerland with plenty to keep him occupied day and night. All he needed was a little time, some distance . . . and a bit of nonthreatening companionship, and he'd soon forget all about an aeronaut with coal-black hair and impossibly blue eyes.

THE BREAKFAST MEETING with the household-products manager had not gone well, and Warren wasted no time in pointing a finger of blame when he and Cole came out of the boardroom.

"Did I really come come across that badly?" Cole asked, already fearing she had.

Warren, the consummate diplomat, took her by the elbow and steered her graciously in the direction of her office. "Cole, sweetie, telling that poor fellow that women's lives do not revolve around retractable floor mops may not be the best approach to use if we hope to land this account."

Cole tugged at the gold hoop in her ear. "Oh, Warren, I was only trying to put things back into perspective, but I can see your point. I don't know what got into me. For some reason, when he made that stupid comment about super-duper retractable floor mops revolutionizing women's lives, I saw red." She stopped outside the door of her office. "Now if you were to show me a self-cleaning floor, I could give you an ad campaign that would set the world on its ear."

Warren chucked her under the chin. "I don't doubt that you would." He turned in the direction of his own office and walked away, shaking his head.

Cole watched him absently for a moment, then opened the door and went to her desk. Last week, she'd been assigned vegetable spinners; this week, retractable floor mops. She knew middle-sized accounts geared to the homemaker were the firm's bread and butter, but it seemed she was getting more than her fair share of them lately. Her patience with dippy product managers and their worthless, cheaply made kitchen gadgets was beginning to wear dangerously thin.

Perhaps she should have a talk with her boss about assigning them to a more junior partner. But as soon as Cole formed a mental picture of Alastair Fawcett, she quashed that idea.

Three weeks! Three whole weeks had gone by without a word from Blackfoot . . . Adam. She wondered if he was still in Switzerland, ballooning or skiing or withdrawing fresh funds from a numbered account. Or perhaps he was back in town. But then, that was a moot point; he hadn't said a word about wanting to see her again.

More than once, Cole had toyed with the idea of calling Adam herself, but there was no listing for a Dr. Adam Torrie in the phone book. In a way, she'd been almost relieved as she'd never had occasion to call a man she wasn't already dating. The very idea turned her bones to jelly.

Or course, she could always ask Warren how to contact him. He'd been so zealous in warning her about the man, though, she could hardly bring herself to admit having fallen headlong into the trap anyway.

Not that she was in love with Adam . . . or even infatuated. Contrary to fairy tales and fables, love did not happen at first sight. No, she was just interested, curious to know something more about the man—well, maybe obsessed was a better word. She felt as if she'd missed the last fifteen minutes of a good mystery movie. When that happened she would stumble around for days afterward, trying to find anyone who had seen the ending. In the meantime, her every waking moment seemed to be spent trying to solve the thing herself. All in all, nothing was ever as satisfying as seeing the outcome firsthand.

Satisfied with having drawn a reasonable comparison, Cole picked up a handful of pencils from her drawer and began to inject them one by one into the electric sharpener. She did have to admit, this whole episode with Adam Torrie was getting out of hand. She had never let a man affect her work like this before, not even during her separation. Then she'd been so furious and so humiliated she'd thrown all her nervous energy into her work. That was what had earned Cole her first promotion. These days, she'd be lucky not to get fired.

A sharp knock on her door brought Cole's aggressive pencil-sharpening campaign to a halt. "Yes?" she called out, grimacing when she pulled out a pencil and saw its point was broken.

"It's just me," said Warren, showing his handsome face around the door.

"Come on in. You're not interrupting a thing."

Warren walked into her office and looked at the pencils strewn across her desk. "If I didn't know better, I'd swear you were inflicting some kind of voodoo curse with those pencils."

Cole had to laugh at his uncanny assessment. "What can I do for you, Warren?"

"Come to my place tonight for Chinese food. My treat." He planted his nice bottom on Cole's desk and began to gather the scattered pencils.

"No, I don't think—"

"Nicole Jameson, if you stay home one more night to wash your hair, there won't be any to wash." To emphasize his point, Warren aimed a sharpened pencil at her throat and fastened his unwavering blue eyes on her.

"Okay, okay," Cole relented, wondering why on earth he would care to have such miserable company for dinner. "But I get the extra shrimp!"

"Deal! See you in an hour."

THERE WAS NO EXTRA SHRIMP. For the first time in history, their favorite Chinese restaurant had sent an even number. Cole slouched on Warren's sofa. The shrimp was just another indication of the nosedive her life had taken lately.

"It's taken me days to figure this out," Warren announced as he refilled their wineglasses, "but I think I finally have it."

"Have what?" Cole was preoccupied with a minute piece of skin on her finger that was threatening to become a hangnail.

"The reason you've been acting like Attila the Hun's running mate."

"Warren, that's an awful thing to say to your best friend."

"It's true, and I'm only telling you because we are best friends. I've never known you to be so . . . off rhythm."

"Off rhythm?" she repeated quizzically, picking up her drink.

"You wore the same suit twice last week."

Cole nearly choked on her wine. "I d-did?"

"You don't have to get so upset. It's a nice outfit, but—"

"Yes, well I've been busy," she countered, "and I haven't had a chance to work out my wardrobe schedule for the month."

Warren gave her a bemused smile. "Bull roar, my dear. It's Blackfoot, isn't it?"

Cole tossed her head. "Don't be silly. I haven't given him a single thought." If she convinced Warren, she might convince herself.

I don't know what ever made me think this would work, thought Warren. These were two stubborn people: one too old to change, the other too afraid. "Why have you refused to go ballooning with me the past three weeks?" he asked.

"Like I told you, I've been busy. Besides, your doctor told you to take it easy for a while. I'm only looking out for your best interests."

"We belong to a club, dimwit. You don't have to fly with me. There'd be plenty of other willing aeronauts." His tone softened to one of real concern. "You're so close to getting your license; you're crazy to let it drop now."

"I'll get back to it!" Cole snapped. "Just drop it, okay?" The wineglass in her hand began to tremble. Damn it! None of this was his fault. "I'm sorry, Warren. You'd be well within your right to toss me out of here. I've behaved like an absolute beast. But you shouldn't worry about me. I'm a big girl now."

Warren reached over and patted her hand then refilled her glass. "I'm just returning a favor. Remember how you helped me get over Charlotte?"

Even Cole's glum spirits couldn't override the memory of Warren's most notorious girlfriend. "How could I forget Charlotte, with the forty-fours and the talons?" she said with a burst of welcome laughter.

Just then there was a knock on the door that sent Cole's mind plummeting back to her own reminiscences. She lay back on the sofa while Warren went to answer the door. If she closed her eyes, she discovered, she could almost relive the sensation of soaring among the clouds beneath a silver and indigo bubble in stillness that was otherworldly, ethereal. She could recall how it felt to share companionship with a strong, taciturn man who somehow didn't fit in with the cosmopolitan rat race of everyday life. . . .

"Blackfoot!" Warren's greeting carried a mixture of warmth and annoyance.

Cole froze, grateful that the back of the couch offered a barrier—albeit temporary—between her and the man who had lately monopolized so many of her thoughts.

But he couldn't have come at a worse time. The tip of her nose always turned pink after the second glass of wine, and she was on her fourth. And though she felt herself to be reasonably in control, who could say what words of fury might leap from her mouth if she dared to open it?

Cole looked down and wiggled her toes. Heaven only knew where she'd left her shoes. Glancing at her skirt of apple-green linen, she realized she'd tossed her jacket somewhere, too. The scoop-necked yellow jersey looked presentable enough, and at least she hadn't dribbled any wine on herself so far.

"How ya doin', old buddy?" she heard Adam say. The sound of his husky voice was as exciting as ever. Obviously, things had gone well for him in Switzerland; he sounded as though he was in particularly high spirits.

"Not bad," Warren replied blandly. "How 'bout you?"

"Pretty good, thanks."

There was a moment or two of awkward silence. Then Cole realized Warren wasn't planning on letting him in. Oh, for heaven's sake, she thought irritably, invite the man in. He wasn't going to bite!

"May I come in?" Adam finally had to ask, echoing Cole's silent command. Then he lowered his voice in an aside. "I haven't come at a bad time, have I? Are you entertaining someone?"

"As a matter of fact..." Warren began, not at all sure that Blackfoot deserved to find out who his guest was.

If ever there was a time, Cole decided, to announce one's presence, this was it! She sat upright a little too quickly and her head began to spin. "Come in, Adam. You haven't come at a bad time."

From the frigid reception she got from the two men, she might have been heralding the second coming of the ice age. Warren and Adam turned in unison to glare at her and the silence in the room was glacial. She had the distinct impression that if anyone spoke the air would shatter into icy little crystals.

"I didn't realize you had company," Adam said after an unbearably long lapse. "I'll come back another time."

"No, don't do that!" Cole insisted rather loudly, as she swung her unshod feet onto the floor and stood up. She counselled herself to move more slowly next time. "I was just leaving anyway." The two of them probably had lots of catching up to do—ribald tales of conquests in the Swiss Alps or some such thing.

Warren was stationed at the door like a cigar-store Indian. "You were not just leaving," he protested.

"And you're in no condition to drive," Adam added in dictatorial tones.

"Yes, I am," Cole said, having every intention of hailing a cab. But she'd sooner crawl home than admit it to him.

"No, you're not," Adam argued.

Cole looked up to glower at him, but the glower soon faded to a gaze. Adam was dressed in snug, faded denims, a pale-blue knit shirt and an aviator jacket of butter-colored chamois. The jacket looked so soft and he looked so . . . fabulous.

Despite the fact that an invitation had not been proffered, Adam made his way past Warren and entered the apartment. He went straight to the coffee table with its remnants of Chinese food, an empty wine bottle and a second one glaringly half empty beside it. "Looks as though a good time was had by all," he remarked dryly.

"I'll take Cole home," was Warren's incongruous response from his post at the door.

Adam reacted to Warren's questionable sobriety with a guffaw. "I wouldn't recommend you do that." He turned to Cole, who stood a few feet away, swaying occasionally. "What do you want to do? Stay and continue your party . . . or go home?"

"Go home," she mumbled, resenting the presumptuous tone in his voice. He had no call to be snide and she hadn't asked for a chauffeur. It wasn't her fault if people insisted on drafting themselves for the job.

"Fine. Let's go, then." Adam reached out and took Cole's wrist, yanking her into some semblance of ambulatory movement.

"I need my shoes," she said, "and my jacket."

"So I see." He scanned the room.

"They're over here," Warren said and pointed to a spot near the door.

Adam led Cole to her pile of belongings then bent down and lifted her foot.

"Hey, what do you think you're doing?" she demanded as he worked her feet deftly into her taupe pumps. Cole's hands flew out reflexively to keep herself from toppling, and they landed squarely on his back. Adam had to stop what he was doing to adjust himself to the added weight.

A smile dallied on Cole's lips. The chamois jacket was as buttery soft as it looked. And Adam's back was hard and strong and warm, just the way she remembered it to be. Were his curls still as crisp? she wondered. With a will of their own, Cole's fingers moved upwards, glossing Adam's neck, burrowing themselves into his thick, curly pelt. Yes, they were still crisp.

Cole watched with amazement as a tremor rippled through Adam's body and his neck flushed a deep shade of cinnamon. He turned his head so that Cole's hand slid to his weather-roughened cheek. "I'd be careful if I were you," he growled in a low voice.

She yanked her hand away as if she had touched an open flame and the sensation lingering along her arm was searing. Yet, far from having learned her lesson, Cole had to battle an irrational urge to touch him once more, just to see if she had imagined the experience.

"Both of you are welcome to stay, you know," Warren said, seemingly unaware of the smoldering exchange between his two friends.

Cole looked up and felt a sudden pang of empathy for Warren. Gorgeous as he was, he seemed to fade beside his friend. She wondered why that was; she had never known Warren to fade beside anyone.

"Thank you, Warren," she said gently, walking over to plant a chaste kiss near his mouth, "but tomorrow's a workday, so I ought to go home and have my hangover tonight. That way, I'll be ready to wage war on a fresh batch of product managers in the morning."

Warren's bleary face eased into a smile. "G'night, Cole."

"Good night, Warren. Thanks for dinner. Next time, it's on me."

Cole scooped up her jacket, crumpled it in one hand and walked through the open door. She didn't bother to check if Adam was following her; she'd just as soon he forget his offer to take her home. Maybe if she got to the elevator quickly enough, she could catch it before he got there.

But no such luck. He was right behind her, moving as swiftly and silently as—as a . . . Blackfoot. His hand reached the elevator button before hers did, and Cole narrowly avoided pressing the nail of his index finger.

Cole remained steadfastly stone-faced and uncommunicative as they descended. What was she supposed to say to him? How was Switzerland? Where the devil have you been for the past three weeks? He had no right to drop in and out of her life like this, as if . . . as if he had never kissed her the way he had that night!

Adam remained irritatingly oblivious to Cole's mood and made no attempt to break the silence. Only when they were in the car, the engine humming, did he turn to her and say, "I had a feeling I'd find you at Warren's."

Cole felt his eyes on her face. Common courtesy dictated that she return the visual contact, but she wasn't feeling very courteous. "I wouldn't have thought so, judging from the stunned look on your face when I sat up," she said, staring straight ahead.

Adam pulled the car away from the curb in a single swift motion. "That's because the first thing I noticed was your nose."

Cole reached up and touched the telltale appendage. Obviously, it was even pinker than usual. "Wine does that to me," she mumbled, sliding lower into her seat.

"No need to explain," he assured her with a casual wave of his hand. "Anyway, I'm glad I found you. I went to your place first, but there was no answer, so I figured I'd try Warren's."

Now Cole turned to stare at him. "Why do you insist on trying to convince me you were at my place first? It doesn't matter to me where you were before you went to Warren's, or where you go next for that matter!" None of which was true, and she knew it . . . but Adam didn't.

"Your *Wall Street Journal* is behind you on the back seat," he countered coolly.

Cole spun her head around to see for herself. "Why'd you steal my newspaper?" she blazed.

"To corroborate my story. But don't worry. I intended to return it to you, one way or another."

She dropped her head back against the seat, temporarily subdued. "How thoughtful of you," she muttered. Like it or not, Cole felt a vague aura of well-being building up inside her, like fluffy white clouds on a summer day. Stubbornly, she refused to give in to the sensation. So he'd been looking for her. So what?

By the time they arrived at her place, Cole's head was pounding and the Chinese food had worn off, leaving her with a queasy, empty feeling in her stomach.

"May I come in for coffee?" Adam asked before she could get a chance to beg off company.

Cole looked at him and shrugged. "Suit yourself," she said and stepped out of the car.

"That's the warmest invitation I've had in months," he said with a laugh, accompanying her up the stairs with the *Wall Street Journal* rolled up under his arm.

Cole's eyes swiveled to his indomitable green ones as she unlocked the door. "Well, what do you expect? You come barging into Warren's unannounced and ruin a perfectly good evening—"

"Now wait just a minute," he admonished, steering Cole inside and closing the door behind them. "I did not barge in. I knocked. And I've known Warren longer than you have, and I've always been welcome there...or almost always." He let the newspaper fall to the floor with a thud. "And as for ruining your evening, I recall you were the one who said she had to leave. What were you so flustered about?"

Without thinking, Cole answered, "I was flustered because we'd just finished talking about you and—" Then she stopped, aghast, and clapped a hand to her mouth too late.

"And?"

Cole shook her head. "Nothing."

"What were you going to say?"

"Never mind!" she cried, her eyes stinging. "It was nothing . . . derogatory." What had she intended to tell him? That she was hurt and angry because he hadn't called, or that seeing him again made her feel even worse than ever?

Adam touched her shoulders lightly. "You're upset with me, Cole. Why?"

Flabbergasted, Cole realized he actually didn't see himself as the culprit in this situation at all. His expression of concern evaporated the last of her anger. Cole pulled away and turned in the direction of the kitchen. "I'm not upset with you," she said in a low voice as she walked away.

Cole disappeared into her small, efficient kitchen and leaned against the counter, willing herself to stay calm with a few deep breaths. What on earth was the matter with her? Adam didn't owe her a thing, and she knew it. There was no reason for her to feel neglected.

She poured a blend of roasted coffee beans into a grinder and watched the pungent beans being pulverized. Adam had come here first, she reminded herself. And for some reason, he'd felt it necessary to prove it to her. That meant something, didn't it?

Several minutes later, Cole appeared in the living room with a tray of coffee and homemade muffins that had journeyed from freezer to microwave to plate in record time. Cole's eyes skimmed over the colorful room with its collection of wooden carvings, set against a background of brightly patterned rugs and rattan furniture in fiery florals. The large bay window let in streams of early-evening light that caught the leaves of her palm tree and weeping fig. She loved this time of the day best, when the room glowed with the aura of a setting from Somerset Maugham.

Adam was standing by the nesting tables, examining one of the carvings. He looked up and smiled. "Whoever carved this one had talent."

The statue he held was of a Caribbean woman with a blanket on her head. Her clothes were tattered and the basket was filled with laundry and a few meager vegetables; but she had the elegant bearing of a queen, her basket a crown.

"Isn't it marvelous?" Cole agreed, smiling, as she set down the tray. "I bought it in Haiti from a wood carver who lived away up in the back hills, miles from the nearest tourist area. His wife was the model."

Adam's interest perked. "And what, may I ask, were you doing in the back hills of Haiti?"

"Shortly after my divorce, I went with a group of friends to the Caribbean where we rented a villa for a couple of weeks. A few of us liked driving around in our rented car, going wherever the roads took us. That's when we found this fabulous artisan. I only wish I had bought more of his pieces. Since then, I've had to content myself with scouring local flea markets to add to my collection."

"Why don't you take more trips?" asked Adam.

Cole picked up the statue and traced its rustic lines with her finger. "I don't know. It's hard to find someone to go with who's willing to spend his or her hardearned dollars on a destination they're not interested in." She smiled wistfully and returned the carving to its place on the table. "I'm glad I took the chance when I did."

"If you pick the place, I'd be happy to accompany you."

He made the offer as casually as if it were an out-of-town picnic. One of the advantages of unlimited finances, Cole surmised. One could afford to be blissfully spontaneous.

Cole glanced at him and went to sit down on the sofa. She could feel Adam's intense eyes following her. "Thanks anyway," she said, "but we're not exactly well enough acquainted to be travel companions. And from what I've heard about your itineraries, you're way out of my league."

Adam came to sit down beside her and lifted an ankle to rest on his leg. The muscles of his thighs were strongly defined against the worn nap of the denim; the hand that rested on his calf was well-shaped and sensitive, despite its ruggedness.

"In that case," he said, "I'll stay right here in Philadelphia."

Cole could feel her heart swell to the point where she could scarcely breathe. "What for?" she asked.

He reached out and grasped a lock of Cole's hair between his fingers. "To get to know you better. I realize I should have called or something in the past couple weeks, but I had some urgent business in Switzerland that's kept me preoccupied for some time. Now that it's out of the way, I feel as though I can get on with my life. I hope that can include seeing more of you."

Cole struggled to resist the subtle sensations of his hand near her face. There were still so many questions that needed answers before she could allow her heart to decide. There were so many it was hard to know where to begin.

"The mayor called you Doctor Adam Torrie," she said at last. "Are you?"

Adam's expression altered, but almost imperceptibly, as though it had moved to an adjacent frame on a film. "I was . . . but I'm not practicing at the moment."

"Why not?"

He took her impertinence well and smiled a slow, sad kind of smile. "Someday, Cole, I hope I can tell you all about myself . . . but not now. I only want to concentrate on the present—today, tomorrow—no promises. Do you think you can trust me enough to do that?"

Cole's first reaction was to object as a matter of principle, because what he was offering was as tangible as a handful of air. Yet something told her there was an elemental goodness and decency to the man, and surely she could allow herself to enjoy that experience for as long as it lasted. What did it matter if Dr. Adam Torrie lost his license to practice medicine . . . or whatever? Did a person have to possess a convenient label, a professional tag for Cole to consider him worthy of her time? Couldn't she just allow herself to get to know . . . Blackfoot?

This was her chance to bail out, to escape the heady, thrilling ride that he was offering her. If she did agree to see him again, she had a strange feeling her life would take on extremes of emotion she'd never even imagined before. She wondered if she could allow herself to trust him.

Cole sought the path of least resistance when she answered softly, "I think I can."

5

COLE WAS STEPPING out of the bathtub, secure in the knowledge that Adam wouldn't be arriving to pick her up for some time, when the door bell rang. She turned her head in the direction of the sound and wrapped herself in a fluffy white bath sheet.

"No, it couldn't be," she protested aloud, and then remembered she hadn't seen the paperboy for several weeks. The door bell rang again. "Coming!" Cole cried out as she snatched her purse from the vanity and flew down the stairs, bubbles slithering along her thighs. She opened the door as far as the chain would allow. "Adam!"

"I couldn't wait . . . so I thought I'd make up for last time," he said, grinning.

"But I'm not even dressed!"

"So I see."

Cole glanced down and saw the towel and her bare shoulders were visible through the open door. With a resigned sigh, she slid the chain across and swung open the door. "You might as well come in then."

He was picking her up for dinner at Twin Elms, the Torrie mansion, but as he stepped inside, Cole saw that he was dressed more like a gardener than the sole occupant. He was wearing a pilot's shirt with flapped pockets and epaulets, dun-colored safari shorts and soft rustically made kidskin shoes. So much for the clingy little black number lying on her bed, Cole thought with chagrin.

"Were you planning to go shopping?" he asked, mouth twitching with amusement as he glanced at Cole's purse tucked under her arm.

"No," she tossed back. "I thought you were the paperboy. How have you managed to survive all these years with such a poor sense of timing?"

Adam shrugged. "Don't know. Guess I wouldn't last long in the nine-to-five world, would I?"

Cole couldn't help but laugh. "That, I would say, is a classic understatement." She held out her arm in the direction of the living room. "Why don't you make yourself at home while I slip into something a little more reliable?" She turned and padded up the stairs, still shaking her head in amazement.

After several minutes of rummaging through her closet, Cole decided on a simple white sundress of Indian cotton, set off by delicate fuchsia embroidery at the bodice and hem. She applied makeup lightly and decided that, except for a pair of fuchsia enamel earrings, further adornment was not needed. Genetic good luck had blessed her with a complexion creamy enough to stand on its own, and lately her eyes, naturally framed by long dark lashes, had taken on an extra dazzle.

When Cole came into the living room, she found Blackfoot browsing at her bookshelf. The rays of the late-afternoon sun caught the back of his legs, accentuating their bronze hue and the steel and whipcord of his muscles. His stance, the slope of his shoulders revealed a man who—dspite his cavalier attitude toward so many things—was at ease with himself, a stranger to pretense and appearances.

After a moment or two, Adam lifted his eyes from the photojournal he'd been perusing. He gave a long, low whistle. "And I thought you looked good in a towel."

Cole flushed with pleasure. "Thank you."

"Shall we go?" he asked, returning the book to its place on the shelf.

"If you like."

The ride to Twin Elms was pleasant, and they chatted about nothing in particular. Cole soon found herself soaring on a light mood that lent sparkle to her conversation and color to her cheeks. It was all she could do to keep her hands in her lap and not reach out to touch the man who so effortlessly evoked high spirits in her.

Cole had seen the Torrie home from the outside on numerous occasions but hadn't paid particular attention to it, dismissing it as another of the many old mansions on which Philadelphia prided itself. She had toured a few of them as a girl, and even then, most of them had struck her as overdone and entirely unlivable.

Adam drove the car through the immense front gates and gave a friendly wave to the security guard. "I don't use the front entrance," he told Cole. "The house is open to the public during the day, so whenever I'm in town I live in a little niche in the back."

"But you will show me the place, won't you?" Cole asked, much to her surprise. But then, this was no ordinary museum; it was Adam Torrie's family home. She was dying to see what it was like.

He gave her a dubious look, then shrugged and drove the car around to the circular drive at the front. Twin Elms was set on ten acres of cultivated grounds. The laws were plush and precisely mown and the box hedges were pruned to resemble birds and fish. The house itself was a monstrosity of Grecian columns, turrets and gargoyles.

Cole must have visibly registered her opinion, for Adam laughed and said, "I know what you're thinking. When I was a kid and we used to visit from Montana the place gave me nightmares. I much preferred the four-room bungalow on the reservation."

They entered through double doors to a magnificent two-story entrance hall with a domed skylight and sweeping staircase.

"I'll take you to what I call the stuffy wing first," he said.

Cole slipped her hand into his and followed him through an immense loggia running over with foliage and statuary. Doors of glass and wrought iron opened onto a formal dining room with a Bohemian glass chandelier and Savonnerie carpets. There was a ballroom with walls of jade green silk and Louis XV furniture, and a salon with intricately painted murals of bacchanalian excess.

"Have you had enough?" Adam asked after they'd covered the balance of the stuffy wing and the entire second floor.

Cole smiled. "I will admit my teeth are beginning to ache, but I don't want to quit until I've seen it all."

Looking at Blackfoot, Cole became acutely aware of the incongruity between him and his birthright. He no more fit into this display of exaggerated wealth than a panther would in a glass menagerie. He was too alive, too vital and earthy to live amid such opulence. In many ways, he was more Blackfoot than Torrie.

They finished the tour by going through the recreational wing, past the bowling alley, the squash court, a Romanesque indoor pool and arriving, finally, at the billiards room.

"Now this is a spot I could settle into quite nicely," Cole remarked, letting her hand graze along the supple leather furnishings. The large imported billiards table was the main attraction, but the room itself was no less impressive. The walls were covered with hand-carved oak paneling, and above a huge stone fireplace hung the Torrie coat of arms. The room was rich, warm and utterly livable.

"It's my favorite room, too," said Adam. "But you're lucky to be in here. In my grandfather's day, it was strictly off-limits to women."

"Ah, yes," Cole mused, her eyes wandering across the lofty beamed ceiling. "Brandy and cigars in here for the gentlemen; port in the parlor for the ladies." She turned to look at Blackfoot. "So where's your little niche? I haven't seen anything that would even remotely fall into that category."

Adam grinned. "Come with me. I'll show you." A glass-and-oak door opened from the billiards room to a large, exotic greenhouse, musky and tropical, with ferns and citrus trees and flowers and palms in riotous growth everywhere. Spreading his arms, he said, "I live in here."

"Oh, come on," Cole replied, laughing. "You don't expect me to believe you live in the greenhouse."

"But I do," he insisted, and led her farther into the heart of the glass enclosure. Finally out of the dense foliage, they came to a gazebo, a charming hexagonal structure of glass and white lattice. "Would you like to see the inside?" he asked.

"Yes, if only to substantiate your claim," she teased.

Sure enough, inside the gazebo was a bachelor's hideaway, in the most delightful setting Cole had ever seen.

"I love it!" she exclaimed, her eyes taking in the brick-and-plant shelves crammed with books. A rustic pine table and chairs; a small sink, fridge and microwave made up the kitchen; the bed was a futon mattress covered with a colorful Navaho-style spread.

Adam looked around with a smile of satisfaction. "Do you? It suits my purposes while I'm in town, and I like the feeling of living in a perpetual jungle." He turned to Cole. "Care to join me in the kitchen? I have to put the vegetables on."

Cole's eyes went to the microwave an arm's reach away.

"Not in here," he said, laughing. "This kitchen's strictly for TV dinners."

In Twin Elm's cavernous kitchen, Cole sat down on a stool to watch Adam assume the role of culinary genius. She'd expected him to throw a couple of steaks on the grill—in the time-honored tradition of male gastronomy—and ask her to toss a salad. It was obvious she was in for something quite extraordinary.

On the stove, a large saucepan was bubbling away with wonderful scents of onion, tomato and pepper, while the oven held promise of yet more delectable surprises. Adam was shaping patties from a mixture destined for the deep fryer, and beside Cole was a platter of assorted condiments: raisins, coconut, chutney, yogurt and a sauce that looked five-alarm hot.

Cole reached over and nabbed a few raisins while Adam wasn't looking. Where had she read that one of these things contained enough food energy for nine kisses? Or was it eleven? She smiled at the absurdity of her thoughts and popped a few raisins into her mouth.

"Are you familiar with African cooking?" Adam asked over his shoulder.

"Not beyond what I've seen on television," replied Cole, "and I never could figure out what the women were grinding in their calabashes."

"Grains mostly," he said and laughed, "but I seem to have misplaced my mortar and pestle, so I've resorted to preground."

"Where did you learn to cook African food?"

Adam lifted the lid from the simmering pot and sampled the broth. "I've spent some time in Liberia, Ghana...Nigeria. I developed a real love for their food and had to learn how to make it for myself. The women thought that was a great novelty, some crazy American wanting to learn women's work, but they were terrific teachers."

Cole took a deep appreciative sniff. "You must have passed your course with flying colors."

"Thanks." He turned his attention to the pumpkin-colored patties turning golden in the fryer. "Would you mind setting the table?" he asked, indicating with his hand which cupboard held the dishes.

"Not at all." She went to the cupboard and took out very functional, everyday china. "Are we eating in here?" she asked, pointing at the large butcher-block table.

"Oh, yeah," Adam answered. "Is that okay with you? I can't stand eating in the dining room. It reminds me of the Astrodome."

Cole looked askance at the kitchen, with the two-hundred-plus cupboards and a mile of counter space. "I know what you mean. Airplane hangars are always cozier than Astrodomes."

"What?" He wiped his hands on the barbecue apron he was wearing. "Oh, I guess I see what you mean. I'm more comfortable in here because it's where I ate breakfast and lunch under the watchful eye of our housekeeper, Miss Lilia. She's been gone over twenty years, but I still feel I have to finish all my vegetables when I'm in this room."

"Smart woman. See how well you turned out?" See, indeed, Cole thought as she watched him bring steaming platters of food to the table. Tall, dark, brimming with good health . . .

Adam brushed off her praise with a hearty laugh. "I think you'll find the meal a little overpowering for wine. I prefer beer with it myself—helps douse the fire. Would you care for some?"

"Why not?" she said, and chuckled at her earlier daydream about candlelight and wine—with the steak and salad, of course—and the two of them seated at an enormous formal dining table, surrounded by austere portraits of Torrie forebears. As she recalled, there were even butlers and maids in her daydream, but so far the only person she'd seen was the security guard. So much for daydreams, Cole thought and held out her mug for Adam to fill. Reality was turning out much nicer anyway.

Adam pulled up a chair beside her at the table and slid a large tureen closer to him. "This is groundnut stew," he explained as he ladled the contents into two bowls.

"Groundnut?"

He nodded. "Try it."

Cole took a spoonful of the thick broth. "Mmm, delicious . . . and—hot!" She waved a hand in front of her mouth until she could quaff some beer to extinguish the effect of the peppers. Afterwards, there was a pleasant, lingering piquancy on her tongue. "It is good, once you've passed the trial by fire."

He seemed pleased. "Groundnuts are peanuts. People use them to supplement their protein supply when meat is scarce."

"What's in here?" Cole asked when she'd finished her stew, lifting the lid from a silver platter.

"Chicken casserole. Add some of the condiments to it, they'll perk up the flavors."

Cole did as she was told and pronounced the casserole excellent. "And how about these cute little orange cakes?"

"Ah, these are my irrefutable favorite. *Ntomo krakro*—yam fritters. The perfect marriage of starch and grease."

She bit into one. "Fabulous. Like hash browns, but sweeter. Did anyone every tell you you'd make someone a fabulous wife?"

Adam shook his head, a mouthful of fritter preventing an immediate reply. "Not lately. Besides, cooking is probably my only spousal virtue, and I don't think it's enough to base a marriage on, from what I'm told."

"Have you never been married?" Cole asked.

Perhaps it was the familiarity of his surroundings or the mellowing effect of the beer, but Adam didn't even flinch at Cole's direct question. "No, but I've been engaged twice."

"No kidding," Cole remarked, leaning forward with her elbows on the table in flagrant violation of Emily Post. "What happened?"

Adam paused and for a moment Cole thought he wasn't going to tell her. He took a sip of beer and leaned back in his chair. "My first engagement was to a pert little Bryn Mawr blonde named Suzi. Just the kind of girl my mother would have picked for me, if she'd been alive."

Cole knew the type. Pretty from the day she was born and incapable of survival without being reminded of her beauty at least once a day. No gawky adolescence for her; just lots of clothes, coming-out parties and an inoffensive liberal-arts degree to while away the time until marrying suitable old money. It was nearly impossible for Cole to imagine Adam in the role of society suitor, yet it was the role he was born in.

"Looking back on it," he went on to explain, "I can see we were just a couple of kids. She ought to be grateful now that I called it off when I did."

"You called it off?" Cole asked, surprised to feel an acute sense of relief over an incident that had occurred decades ago.

Adam nodded. "Guess life on a reservation had a pretty strong effect on me. I called it off the day I walked into Suzi's house and found her in hysterics because the caterer wanted to use silver-plated napkin rings for the reception instead of sterling."

Cole nearly sprayed a mouthful of beer across the table in an effort to control her laughter. "You broke the engagement over napkin rings? She must have been furious!"

"Livid. The following year she married a stock-broker, and they have two children who are virtual delinquents. I'm sure she's happy." By the way he laughed, Cole knew there was no love lost for poor old Suzi.

"What about your other engagement?" But the moment she'd asked the question, Cole wished she could take it back. The anguish that flashed across Adam's face was brief, but it was obvious the scars ran deep. "If you'd rather not talk about it . . ." she offered.

He brushed it off. "No . . . it's all right. I don't mind talking about it anymore. She was an Egyptian girl . . . a nurse."

Egyptian? Images of Cleopatra and Nefertiti passed through Cole's mind, and suddenly she felt awkward and dowdy. "What was her name?" she asked. She had to know.

"Atalaya."

"How beautiful," Cole said softly, though she was disturbed by the jolt of jealousy that ran through her. It wasn't right for her to feel that way; Adam was entitled to a life before he met her. She'd been married herself, after all. "Where is she now?" Cole forced herself to ask.

"She's dead. Soon after we became engaged, she volunteered for Red Cross duty in Syria. She was killed by a sniper less than a month after she arrived."

Adam's pain ripped through Cole's heart like barbed wire. "Oh, I'm sorry," she said softly, and reached across the table for his hand.

His eyes glittered overbright for only an instant then mirrored quiet resignation. "It's been eight years. Time makes the pain and the memories fade." He took his fingers from her hand and moved them along the delicate bones of her wrist. "You remind me of her in some ways."

Cole didn't know how to feel. Part of her resented being compared to the ghost of Atalaya, who would remain forever young and flawless in Adam's mind. But part of her was flattered, for if a man like Adam had loved Atalaya, then surely she was a worthy and remarkable woman. If she envied anything, it was the love Atalaya had been lucky enough to experience.

When Cole lifted her eyes to meet Adam's, a river of sympathy and understanding flowed between them, transcending the harsh realities of the past. She longed to put her arms around him, to soothe away the bitter memories. Her entire body ached to feel his head against her breast, her fingers in his curls. But here in the harsh unrelenting light of the kitchen she had to content herself with the intimacy to be found in his deep green eyes.

"What do you say to coffee and dessert in the billiards room?" he asked, severing their brief and fragile contact by pushing himself away from the table.

"Sounds wonderful," she replied, feeling as though she'd just come closer than ever to the deep inner workings of Adam Torrie. She'd flown past him as if on a trapeze, touching him briefly from dizzying heights and sailing on . . . hoping, waiting to swing back and touch him once again.

Adam brought her to the oak-paneled room and switched on a pair of silk-shaded lamps above the billiards table. "Wait here," he said. "I'll be back in a minute with the coffee."

Okay, Blackfoot, this is your chance, he told himself as he returned to the kitchen to assemble the dessert and pour the coffee. For weeks, he'd been waiting to exact satisfaction from Cole for complicating his deliberately uncomplicated sex life. The woman might as well have been perched on his shoulder the entire time he was in Switzerland, taunting him with the memory of her untried charms. So, if the seduction of Cole Jameson was what it would take to get his life back on course, then that's what he had to do.

It wasn't as though he had a hard road ahead of him. He hadn't been away from the real world so long that he didn't recognize desire when he saw it. There had to be something in this tired old body of his that made Cole's eyes light up the way they did and made her hands move around as if they needed somewhere to go.

The corners of Blackfoot's mouth lifted in a grin as he brought the espresso and dessert to the billiards room. When it came right down to it, Cole made him feel twenty all over again. Now to find out if she could make the feeling last!

COLE TOOK THE DISH of figs and honey from Adam and the side of his hand brushed against hers. Her eyes flew wide open at the startling contact. He returned her gaze without flinching, yet she felt as though his eyes were somehow roving all over her body, laying claim to all he surveyed.

With great effort, she pulled her eyes away and looked down at the plate in her hands. "Figs," she said. "I love figs."

"Do you? It's an Egyptian dessert."

Cole wondered why he would say something like that, and with such an odd challenging tone of voice. She replied without the slightest malice. "Did Atalaya teach you how to make it?"

There was a glimmer of remorse in Adam's expression. He placed his own dessert on the coffee table and closed the distance between them on the sofa. "I'm sorry, Cole. I didn't mean to bring her up."

"That's all right. Obviously, you still care for her a great deal."

He shook his head. "That part of my life is over. I hadn't even thought about her for years . . . until you came along."

Cole turned her head away. "Are we that much alike?"

"No! Damn it, this isn't coming out right at all."
Adam took Cole's untasted dessert from her hands, set
it aside and brought her face around to his. "Let me try
again. There are a few similarities between you and
Atalaya. Your black hair, your firebrand tempera-
ment, but beyond that you're two very different
women. She came into my life when I was young and
brash and full of idealistic notions. She was able to cure
me of many of those ills. But now I'm older—not a hell
of a lot wiser—and there isn't much that gets my blood
stirring anymore. Until I met you, that is . . ." His eyes
slipped down along Cole's body to make his point even
more effectively. Then he lowered his head to kiss the
side of her neck.

"Oh, Adam . . ." Cole moaned, but no further response would come. All of her thoughts, all of her
senses had rallied to the pulse point at her neck where
his lips were softly caressing her.

"Cole," he murmured. His voice was dark with desire as his arms came around her waist and he brought
her body to his. A low, husky groan escaped his throat
the moment their lips met. Cole could easily equate that
sound with her own wrenching need.

It had been three weeks since she last tasted his kisses
yet in some ways it seemed like forever. She shifted her
lower body closer; her breasts were crushed against his
chest. When her lips parted, Adam delved into her
mouth with the hunger of a man too long denied; yet
he was gentle, his lips full and pliant while his fingers
moved through her hair, caressing the silky black locks.

Then he lifted his mouth from hers and searched her
face with scorching intensity. What he was seeking,

Cole couldn't begin to guess. All she knew was that her lips were throbbing and she couldn't bear the distance between them any more than she could bear the painful, questioning look in his eyes. She grasped his curls with one hand and returned his mouth to hers, bearing down on his lower lip, skimming his mouth tantalizingly with the tip of her tongue.

Adam, barely severing the kiss, lifted Cole effortlessly in his arms and lay her down on the supple leather sofa. He brought himself down to lie with her and Cole's entire body shivered in response, her lush breasts rising and falling with each fevered breath, reveling in the sensations of Adam's hard and virile body aligned with hers.

With all rational thought abandoned, all uncertainty cast aside, Cole threw her head back. Adam's lips left her face and trailed kisses along her neck, setting off alarms at touch points that aroused her entire body.

His hands slid beneath the straps of her sundress and eased them over her shoulders. "Cole," he rasped. "What have you done to me?" He lowered his eyes and gazed almost worshipfully at the gentle slope of her bare shoulders. He tasted her skin and his breath ignited the sensitive area where her breasts began to swell.

The elastic on the bodice of Cole's sundress gave way without a struggle, and she arched back to allow the fabric to slip to her waist more easily. In the next moment, her breasts lay bare, golden in the soft light. As Adam gazed on her, she felt her nipples spring to life. The moment seemed so fragile, Cole scarcely dared breathe.

Then she thought she saw him shake his head and he shut his eyes just for an instant. She felt her full breasts aching for his touch . . . Why wasn't he touching her?

At last, Adam moved his hand up from Cole's waist, took her breast, and covered it with his warmth. Sensations radiated from the taut peaks like ripples in a pond, spreading through Cole's body in ever-widening circles as he caressed her with tender agility.

"I can't . . ." she heard him murmur, and Cole stiffened in alarm.

What was he saying? He couldn't do this to her—bring her this far and not see it through! Cole grasped his head with both hands and brought him to her aching breasts; she didn't need to do more. Adam's mouth found the swollen bud and knew precisely how to assuage its needs. With an expert hand, he massaged her other breast until he came to it and applied equally attentive measures.

"You are so beautiful, Cole . . . you take my breath away." He turned his head to one side and lay it in the valley between her breasts. His breath came in shallow, labored gasps, and Cole knew he was holding back. She could sense the vibrations of his struggle in her own body.

"Please don't stop," she entreated gently, wrapping her arms around his neck.

As if responding to some inexplicable resolve, he ignored her plea. He brought his hands to her shoulders and lifted his face to hers. Longing had deepened the lines on his brow and stained his eyes a turbulent shade of malachite. "It won't work," he said as he slid Cole's dress back into place. Before she could reply, he was on his feet, staring down at her. "This was a big mistake, bringing you here tonight," he said in a bitter, almost savage voice. "I can't make love to you!"

6

COLE SAT UP, fumbling with the bodice of her sundress. She could feel splotches of color heating her skin, but she needn't have worried that Adam would notice. He was stalking back and forth in front of the stone fireplace, his eyes blazing a trail ahead of him. The room was charged with conflicting energies, desire colliding with repudiation, indignation with concern.

"What do you mean, you can't make love to me?" Cole finally managed to ask, her voice tremulous.

Adam pushed his fingers through his curls, an almost angry gesture. "I don't expect you to understand this, Cole, but things . . . have progressed a little too quickly between us. I think it's best if we . . ." His voice trailed off.

Either his convictions were wavering, or he was trying to think of a humane way to break it to her, Cole thought in confusion. "If we never see each other again?" she offered. "Is that what you were trying to say?" Even as she spoke, she unwittingly continued to relive the feel of his mouth on hers, his tingling kisses on her breasts. She dug magenta nails into the leather of the sofa and drew in a deep ragged breath.

Adam turned to her, his face drawn and impossible to read. "No, that's not what I was going to say. But we ought to let our relationship cool down a bit, put some distance between us."

Cole bit her lip. "I see. Is there something you're not telling me that you should be telling me?"

"If you mean am I gay or carrying something communicable, the answer is no."

She should have felt relieved instead of disappointed. "Do you have some sort of...problem?" Cole asked as delicately as she could.

Adam gave a bitter laugh. "No, Cole, as far as I know, I'm not impotent."

His bluntness caught her off guard, but she pressed on. "Then what—"

"Cole, please, no more questions! I'm tired, I've got jet lag and I've done a lion's share of confessing tonight. More than I've done with anyone for a long time."

His eyes were pleading. Cole sensed that he needed her tacit understanding and she longed to give it to him. She could almost feel her own discomfiture slip away as she looked into his tortured eyes. It would be so easy to take his hand, lead him to the couch and do nothing but talk until dawn, if that's what he wanted to do. They would grow close in a safe, caring way that wouldn't leave emotions exposed, raw and vulnerable.

But part of her—a long-hidden, almost alien part of her—dismissed such notions as the coward's way out. Something inside her wanted to break loose from its protective tethers and soar to new, uncharted sensual heights. Her husband had been a cold man, detached and perfunctory in his lovemaking. For years, Cole had blamed herself, and no other man had gotten close enough to prove her wrong.

No one, that is, until Adam. One lingering gaze from him was all it took for Cole to trust him, one touch kindled her desire. And she knew—knew as surely as the sky is blue—that it would take only one night in his arms for her to give her heart away completely.

All of which was irrelevant. He didn't want her. And the plain, unvarnished truth of the matter was you couldn't make someone want you. Cole stood up on unsteady legs. "I think I'll go home now."

Adam made a move toward her. "Let me drive you."

"No-no, thank you. I'll just take a cab." She needed to be alone soon, before tears of frustration gave her away.

"Then let me at least give you the money," he countered gently.

Cole flinched. She picked up her purse and turned to face him. "I may not be an heiress, Blackfoot, but I can still afford my own taxi fare," she ground out, trying not to notice the flash of pain that crossed his face.

"Don't be angry, Cole," he said quietly, jamming his fists into the front pockets of his shorts. He looked very vulnerable standing there.

"Angry?" Cole echoed, her voice a trifle shrill. "I'm not angry. Why should I be? You invite me here for dinner, you stage a pass like any other normal, warm-blooded American male and then, just when your path is clear, you change your mind." Cole hooked a finger into the strap of her purse and swung it over her shoulder. "You see, I suffer from a rather annoying handicap. I was one of those foolish girls who married the only boy she'd ever dated right after high school. While most of my peers were off battling the sexual revolution, I was clipping coupons and reading *Family Circle*. I'm still trying to get past the old playing-hard-to-get routine. I guess it shows." She turned on one heel and headed toward the door.

Adam's reaction was a groan of empathy that made Cole freeze in her tracks. "Don't talk about yourself like that," he said. "I want you very much, and I'm not interested in a résumé with experience either."

She wasn't sure what kept her from running right back into his arms—he still seemed as much a refuge as a deep, dark mystery—but she kept walking, the click of her heels feigning determination. "Yes, well...I really must go. Thanks for dinner."

"I'll call you..."

Cole whirled around, her face set despite shimmering eyes. "Don't bother!" Regretting her outburst, Cole gave her best rendition of a casual grin. "Please...leave me with a little pride, would you? We hard-boiled ad-executive types have an image to maintain and, frankly, mine doesn't stand up well to a lot of tinkering." She lifted her fingers in a wave. "Be seeing you." Cole turned on one heel and left the room. This time, Adam did not try to stop her.

Safely ensconced in the back of a taxi, Cole rested her head against the seat and waited for the tears to come, but there weren't any. She sat up and looked around as if she had somehow misplaced them. This was unheard of: Cole Jameson enduring blatant rejection without crumpling into an emotional heap. Feeling almost cheated, she replayed the scene at Twin Elms in her mind once more. It was no use; she still didn't feel like crying.

The truth didn't dawn on her until she got home. Scrubbing off her makeup and staring dry-eyed at the bathroom mirror, she realized what was missing. Self-abnegation, Warren the amateur therapist labelled it. Cole's lifelong habit of blaming herself for every little mishap, every breakdown in communication between herself and others.

"What am I doing wrong?" she used to shriek at her husband. "Just tell me what it is, and I'll work on it!" So he'd dredge up an irrelevant shortcoming or two—probably because she wouldn't leave him in peace until he did—and she'd spend the next few weeks dismally striving for perfection. All to no avail, of course. Her husband hadn't wanted things to be better; he'd already been sleeping with his secretary for months.

Cole knew she had come close to repeating her mistakes tonight with Adam. That comment about the sexual revolution had definitely smacked of the old ways, but he had stopped her in time, refusing to listen. He might not have been ready to open up to her yet, but at least he hadn't let her leave with a pile of misplaced guilt.

Now what kind of a man would voluntarily sacrifice his own satisfaction when there was a woman so handy, just ripe for the picking? Cole slipped into a white satin nightgown and crawled under the sheets. A man she could fall in love with, she answered herself with a smile.

LIBERATION AND INDEPENDENCE ASIDE, it still took Cole a week to garner enough courage to call Adam. She hadn't gone so far as to give any thought to why she was calling or what she'd say when he answered. Too much advance planning and she'd probably chicken out altogether.

She'd been staring at her telephone for fifteen minutes. The scrap of paper with Adam's unlisted number on it was crumpled beyond recognition in Cole's fist, but it didn't matter as the number had lodged itself permanently in her memory the instant Warren had given it to her.

She dialed and waited. One ring ... two rings ... three ... He wasn't home. . . .

"Hello?"

It was him. Her heart stopped. All of Cole's witty conversational gambits, so instantly retrievable with clients, scattered as she faced the awesome reality of Adam's deep husky voice.

"H-hello, Adam?" Aghast, she slapped her hand to her mouth. She had sounded just like a mouse!

"Who is this?"

Maybe if she just hung up ... *No, pretend he's a client. Give him your best Lauren Bacall.* "It's Cole. Cole Jameson." There, that was much better.

"Oh, Cole, hello! I didn't recognize your voice. Must be a bad connection. How've you been?"

"Just fine, thanks," she replied, feeling decidedly faint. He actually sounded pleased to hear from her. Inanely, Cole wondered whether he could hear her thumping heart through the receiver. She could always say there was a *National Geographic* special on TV with drums in the background. "How are you?"

There was a pause. "Getting by. I know you told me not to bother calling you, but I guess I should have . . . under the circumstances."

"It's all right," Cole said, determined not to latch onto his apology as if she was a drowning seaman. "I've worked a lot of evening hours this week. Tonight's the first chance I've had to put my feet up."

"Oh, yeah? I've been kinda busy myself out at my farm. I'm getting ready for the French race."

Cole's interest perked. "Really? Have you been doing some flying?"

"Some, but mostly I've been working on the new balloon for the race."

"You're building your own balloon?" Cole asked, intrigued. An odd vision of Beethoven conducting his own symphonies flashed through her mind.

"I'm taking a stab at it," Adam replied with a modest chuckle. "What started off as a romantic notion has turned out to be one hell of a lot of work."

"That's fascinating! I've never seen a balloon being built." Even to herself she sounded wistful.

Another pause crackled across the wires. "Would you like to help out? I can use another pair of hands . . . and the company."

Cole opened her mouth to cry, "I'd love to!" but stopped herself in time. Was her memory terminally addled? Here she was—eyes wide open, heart wide open—all set to leap into the fire again, without so much as a moment's consideration. At the very least, there had to be some ground rules laid out first.

"I've missed you, Cole."

The scrap of paper in Cole's fist was rapidly disintegrating to soggy pulp. That's what a person got for being impulsive, she remonstrated to herself. She had no contingency plans for the phrase, "I've missed you." Determined to throw a wet blanket over her smoldering enthusiasm, Cole countered with, "Then I guess you should have called."

"I know, but I had a lot of thinking to do . . . about the two of us."

Cole drew in a sharp breath and shut her eyes. "And did you come to any conclusions?"

"A few," Blackfoot admitted. "I'd like to see you again; I'd like us to be friends."

Friends. The word fell on Cole's ear like a lump of wet dough, as would one of those dubious forms of praise akin to having a nice personality or being loved like a sister. How could he ask that of her when he knew how attracted she was to him? She only had to think about their evening at Twin Elms and her whole body tingled in reminiscence. No, friendship was a nice idea, and she'd even entertained the notion herself for a time; but it was impossible.

At that moment, fate reared its intrusive little head, turning Cole's eyes in the direction of a sweet, corny paperweight on her telephone table, a gift from Warren. She groaned. The object lesson couldn't have been any clearer. Warren had been her best friend for as many years as he'd been in love with her. There had to be some sort of divine intervention at work here, she decided with a sigh.

"Okay," she said. "When would you like me to come out to the farm?"

Adam let out a sound of relief. "Tomorrow morning. As early as you care to make it."

Cole picked up a pencil, wondering what Adam would say if he knew about the wild, spiraling sensations orbiting her body at the mere thought of seeing him again. "So how about some directions to this place?" she asked.

SHORTLY AFTER DAWN the next morning, Cole awoke feeling more alive and exhilarated than she had in a week. She showered, dressed and gulped down a bran muffin, juice and coffee, foregoing the usual routine of chewing each mouthful twenty-eight times. Her gastric juices, she decided, were probably as revitalized as the rest of her. Soon she was speeding along the expressway in her little white sports car en route to Adam's farm.

The sun cast diamonds on the dew that covered the passing greenery. Farmhouses set in stands of tall trees gleamed pristine white, and the land undulated in variegated green and gold. Summertime did rural Pennsylvania justice, Cole thought, humming softly as she drove.

As a protective measure, Cole tried everything humanly possible to keep her exuberance in check. Passing the small, picturesque towns of Kimberton and Glenmoore, she tried to concentrate on the ad campaign she'd been working on all week for a new health-food bar. Nutritious and satisfying, it had no sugar or chocolate, yet was every bit as gooey, sticky and sinfully rich as any chocolate bar on the market. The project was a godsend; the product was guaranteed to appeal to kids, moms, health-food types and even closet junk-food nibblers.

Cole had never been a compulsive eater herself. Whenever she became depressed or anxious, she'd either exercise or brush her teeth, whichever was more convenient. But, for some strange reason, this past week she had suffered from the most excruciating craving for chocolate she'd ever known. She would have been genuinely alarmed had it not been for the generous supply of mock chocolate bars her client had given her. As it turned out, her work had never been more inspired.

At last, Cole came to a bend in the highway and there she saw the white clapboard farmhouse with the unicorn weather vane, set away from the road by a huge front yard. Not much resemblance between this place and Twin Elms, Cole thought, as she slowed the car and turned into the gravel driveway. Climbing roses and grapes were given free rein at the sides of the house and hedges were allowed to grow normally, without being pruned to resemble birds and fish. One wouldn't feel like a museum display living here.

After Cole had parked her car and only a robin or two came to greet her, she walked up a flagstone path to the large screened veranda at the front of the house. She opened the door and stepped inside. There was a rustic porch swing at one end and beside it a pile of newspapers on top of a rickety rattan table. At the other end of the porch was a table positively groaning with flowering begonias, each striving to outdo the other for sheer brilliance of color. It was the homiest place she'd ever seen. Cole was smiling to herself when she knocked on the door.

"Be right there!" a voice called from another room. A moment later, a spunky gray-haired woman bustled to the door, wiping her hands on her gingham apron. "Hello, hello!" she cried with genuine pleasure as she swung the door open. "You must be Miss Jameson."

"Call me Cole," she answered warmly, stepping into an old-fashioned parlor complete with grandfather clock, handcarved rocker and comfortable over-stuffed furniture.

"Pleased to make your acquaintance, Cole," the woman said, holding out her work-roughened hand and shaking Cole's vigorously. "You can call me Hes-ter, Hester Sims." She stepped back and planted two fists firmly on ample hips and looked Cole over with keen, inquisitive eyes. "My, my, Adam was sure enough right about you."

"He-he was?" Cole asked hesitantly. "Why? What did he say?"

"We-ell, I wouldn't want to give you no swelled head or nothin', but he said you were the prettiest thing he'd ever seen, and I'd have to agree with him there. I swear you have eyes the same color as a bunch of morning glories I planted once."

Cole blushed like a schoolgirl and her heart seemed to flip right over. She couldn't think of a thing to say except to murmur a demure thank-you.

Hester gestured for Cole to follow her down the hall to a large cheery kitchen and then out the back door. "Adam told me to bring you straight to the barn. Even though I said to him you'd be hot and thirsty after that long ride in the car, he wouldn't hear tell of you havin' no coffee break before you set off to workin'. So help me Hannah, that boy don't even know when to take it easy, and he expects all the rest of us to follow suit!"

Cole swallowed a grin. She suspected Hester Sims worked just as hard, if the profusion of flowers and the smell of fresh baking were any indication.

On their way, they met a man who looked about Hester's age carrying two pails full of peat moss.

"Jake!" Hester shouted, apparently out of necessity. The man cocked his head and peered quizzically. "This here's Adam's lady friend, Cole Jameson!" Hester turned to Cole and said in a somewhat gentler shout, "This here's my Jake!"

Jake clamped a pair of twinkling gray eyes on Cole and gave her a grin rife with mischief. "So you're Adam's lady friend, eh? 'Bout time he got himself settled down with a wife. It ain't right for nobody to live his life the way he does, year in, year out, always—"

"Jacob Sims, you cut that out!" Hester chided fiercely.

"What's all the shouting about?" Adam came toward them from the barn. He was dressed in paint-splattered jeans and a plaid work shirt, the sleeves rolled to his elbows.

Cole could have curled up with embarrassment, but she was too caught up with seeing Adam again. She'd almost forgotten how rugged and indomitable he looked, and his smile was positively heart-warming. Of course, he'd heard the entire exchange between her and the Simses—they'd have heard it in Pittsburgh—but he was probably used to their direct ways.

"It's nice to see you again, Cole," he said, stopping somewhat abruptly several feet away from her.

"Hello, Adam." She gave him a friendly, noncommittal smile.

"I see you've already met Jake and Hester."

"A fine girl, Adam, a fine girl!" chirped Hester before Cole could reply.

Adam looked down at the older woman and pulled her to his side with filial affection. "And how would you know that? I'll bet she hasn't been here five minutes and hasn't gotten a word in edgewise."

Hester wriggled out from under his muscular arm with an impatient sniff. "I can tell by lookin' at her, that's how! You don't get to be my age without learnin' a thing or two about people, you know!"

"Come along now, woman," Jake rumbled, recovering his buckets and jerking his head in the direction of the vegetable garden. "Let's leave these young folks be. Don't you remember how we were at their age?"

His mate gave him a swat on the arm but nonetheless followed reluctantly behind him. "Y'all holler when you want lemonade, y'hear?" Hester called over her shoulder.

Adam turned and looked at Cole a long while, as if satisfying a healthy thirst. "So what'd you think of Jake and Hester?"

Cole smiled. She'd never seen Adam look so relaxed, so sure of himself, except perhaps when they were on board *Stargrazer*. "They're wonderful. Refreshingly straightforward, aren't they?"

Adam responded with a hearty laugh. "It seems you got their seal of approval. I knew you would." He seemed quite content to just continue looking at her.

"So! Shall we get to work?" Cole asked, clapping her hands together, eager to get onto neutral territory.

"Sure, why not?" he said, grinning knowingly. He brought her to the barn nearby. The large double doors were propped open, and inside it looked like the site of a giant quilting bee. Large swaths of indigo and silver fabric hung from all the rafters and the barn floor was covered with protective plastic. Several strips of indigo nylon were lying on the plastic, ready to be joined together. At the far end of the room, a wooden gondola was beginning to take shape.

"You've done a lot already," Cole remarked.

Adam bent down to remove his work boots, so Cole did the same with her sneakers. "I suppose I have, but it doesn't seem like it." He made a sweeping gesture with his hand. "Today we start joining the pieces. I've opened all the doors and windows and installed fans. The adhesive is pretty strong stuff."

"Don't you sew the pieces together?" Cole asked.

"Nope. Can't risk seams with needle holes." He led her to the center of the room where two large pieces of nylon shaped like orange sections lay side by side. "I've outlined the seam allowances. We apply the adhesive within these lines, then we'll glue a narrow inner strip along the seam for added safety."

"That makes me feel better," Cole quipped, then quickly clamped her mouth shut. She wasn't going to be in the race! Why did that immutable fact never seem to penetrate? Perhaps she had made a mistake in coming here at all. . . . No, that wasn't the right way to look at it, she told herself sternly. Adam needed her help, and friends did not renege on their offers of assistance. "So where would you like me to start?" she asked brightly.

His appreciative look was heartwarming enough to justify a month of slave labor. "Just pick up a brush and start gluing."

Together, they began applying the adhesive and were soon ready to join the first two strips. The work was painstaking because the neoprene-coated nylon was so slippery and awkward to work with, but Cole soon caught the knack of handling the pieces herself and insisted that Adam go back to work on the gondola. She suspected that was where he'd rather be, but that he was too polite to leave the routine work to her. She didn't mind; she was happy just being there.

"I didn't know the Torries were farmers," she remarked, dipping her brush into the glue pot.

"They weren't. The farm came from my mother's family."

"Have Jake and Hester been here long?"

"As long as I can remember. I can't imagine the place without them, even though I know they won't be around anymore when I retire."

Cole chuckled. "Retire? You have to be employed before you can retire."

Adam ceased planing for a moment. "Yeah, you're right. I guess what I meant was, when I get too old and stiff to do anything else, I'll just come out here and spend the rest of my days on the porch swing."

They worked all day. Hester popped in now and again with cold drinks. At noon, their labors were rewarded with a picnic under a lovely old apple tree.

By late afternoon, Cole's muscles and joints were beginning to voice their discontent. Every stroke of the brush was an effort, and she had one giant ache that stretched from her heels to the back of her neck. She nearly cried with relief when Adam laid down his hammer and said, "Why don't we call it quits for the day?"

Cole looked up with a grimace. "Are you sure? I was just getting the hang of it." She tried to stand up. "Oh . . . my gosh! I think I'm going to be permanently shrimp shaped."

He rushed to her side. "Here, let me help."

He held out his hand, but Cole was almost reluctant to reach for it. It seemed reckless; they hadn't touched all day. But then, it was only an innocent offer of help, after all. There was no need to read ulterior motives in everything. She put her hand in his and slowly began to straighten out from her stooped position, cracking and snapping and creaking as she rose. She gave him a rueful look. "You wouldn't happen to have a stretching rack handy, would you?"

Much to her surprise, Adam's eyes glinted devilishly. "I have something even better." Cole yanked her hand away as if she'd been scalded. So much for her naive assumptions.

She hobbled along behind him and winced with embarrassment when she had to let him help her with her shoes. "Do you get the feeling this is becoming something of a habit?" she asked.

Adam merely grinned as he coaxed her heel into the canvas shoe. "There does seem to be some kind of pattern developing."

He took her outside behind the barn and led her down a gently sloping hill. At the bottom was a small lake surrounded by a stand of tall trees. The water was clear and shimmering.

"Oh, it's beautiful!" Cole exclaimed. "Like a watercolor."

"That's where I learned to swim. Jake threw me in one day, and I blubbered and sputtered my way into a half-decent dog paddler." He slid Cole a sideways glance. "You swim, don't you?"

"Sure, but I didn't bring a suit."

"Doesn't matter," he said with a wave of dismissal. He strode along the base of the hill and Cole followed, since she wasn't sure what else to do. "The lake stays cold all year round," he went on to say. "We'll have to warm up first."

Cole shook her head in confusion. "I hope you don't think I'm going to join you in some kind of aerobic workout, and I've never been skinny-dipping in my life!" she warned, scampering along behind him.

Adam didn't even bother to reply. Finally, at the bottom of the hill, Cole saw the small red building tucked away among the trees, smoke curling gently from its chimney. "A sauna?" she asked, relieved.

"The perfect remedy for cranky joints." The corners of his mouth played with a smile. "Especially when followed by a cool, refreshing dip."

Cole stared at him. "No dips!"

He gave her a look of mock gravity. "I was just kidding about that part."

He pushed open the door to the sauna and Cole followed him in, only half convinced she was doing the right thing. In fact, she'd have refused altogether if she hadn't thought she might seize up in the car on her way home and drive into a ditch.

The dressing room was as homey as the farmhouse, though spartanly furnished with cedar benches and braided rugs. The smell of wood smoke was a balm. Still, Cole remained on her guard. "There appears to be only one dressing room," she uttered dryly.

"Well, what did you expect?" Adam answered with a laugh. "This isn't the Hilton."

Cole folded her arms, refusing to be placated.

"Okay." Adam relented. "Why don't we make a pact?" He went to the pile of towels on a nearby bench and divided them in two. He placed one half on either side of the room, as far apart as possible. "There, you undress over here, and I'll undress at that end of the room. We can both promise not to peek."

Cole regarded him suspiciously for a long while, but he seemed to be quite serious . . . except for a questionable spark in the deepest recesses of his green eyes. But there didn't seem to be any way around the situation. "Okay," she agreed.

Adam nodded then crossed the room. With his back toward her, he began to unbutton his work shirt. It took Cole a moment or two to realize she wasn't supposed to be standing there staring at him. With a dubious sniff, she turned and began to undo the buttons of her own lilac cotton blouse. She folded it neatly, then lifted each leg in turn to remove her knee socks. These she placed carefully under the bench. She slipped out of her lilac working shorts then unclasped her bra and let it slide down her arms. As she bent to remove her lace panties, an involuntary shiver raced along her limbs.

Pact or no pact, it was impossible to forget that she wasn't alone in the room. Less than ten feet away, Adam was in some stage of undress.

Cole shivered again and wrapped her arms around herself as she looked around for her towel. It was off to her left, just beyond the limits of her peripheral vision. She wouldn't be able to reach it without turning toward Adam.

It didn't occur to Cole until much later that her feet were not nailed to the floor. She could have taken one step backward and picked up the towel without turning around at all. But suffering as she was from a mild case of tunnel vision, Cole leaned forward and twisted at the waist. As she reached out to grab the towel, her hair fell across her face, but not quickly enough to conceal the sight of Adam. He was totally and gloriously naked.

Cole snapped to attention and knew she ought to feel properly naughty. But she couldn't help it if her mind had snapped a mental picture of his marvelous body, one she could now linger over leisurely. There wasn't anything she could do to block out the image of his tawny back, broad and tapered; his fine, strong thighs covered with silky brown hair; and his buttocks, firm and perfectly proportioned, set off by the tan line from his swimming trunks.

She wrapped the towel around herself and was shocked to feel the thick nap graze over her aroused nipples. Glancing down, she wondered precisely when it was that she'd lost her self-control. She'd had it just a few minutes ago.

"Are you decent?" Adam called out from his corner.

Cole blushed shamelessly. "I suppose." She turned slowly to find Adam properly covered from the waist down.

His eyes dipped briefly to her cleavage then moved back up. "I've never known anyone who can do such justice to an ordinary towel."

Cole recalled ruefully that this wasn't the first time she'd had occasion to wear one in front of him. "Maybe that's because white is my best color."

Adam laughed and opened the door to the steam room, inviting Cole to enter first. She stepped inside and the heat wrapped around her like a second skin. She felt as though a million unseen fingers were massaging her as she moved through the room and climbed up to the highest bench.

Adam picked up a dipper and tossed water onto the hot rocks. "I'll fix you a pan of cool water," he said. "You'll need it soon.

Sooner than you may think, my dear man, thought Cole, stifling a giggle. It was sheer luxury to be able to watch Adam as he bent over the taps and let water gush into the rustic enamel pans. Each time he moved his arm, the muscles of his back rippled; the heat was transforming his body to a glossy shade of russet. Cole had a delicious urge to run her hand over his sleekness.

When the pan was full, he picked it up and rose to his feet. He turned around, caught Cole's eyes, and it was as if he could read her every wanton thought. He stood so still, unblinking, that Cole actually began to entertain the thought of making a full confession.

"You remind me of someone Gauguin would have loved to paint," he said.

Caught off guard by the remark, Cole blushed. "Gauguin . . . he's the one who did those voluptuous Tahitian women, isn't he?"

"Uh-huh. Too bad I haven't got a shred of talent. With your black hair, those remarkable blue eyes and the way your skin glows . . ."

Cole lifted her hands and rolled her eyes skyward. "Yes, well, I've often been told I perspire nicely." The man never ceased to amaze her. One minute he was as forbidding as a brewing storm; the next, open and refreshing. There was so much about him she didn't know . . . so much she wanted to know. It took her ages to realize Adam was holding out a pan of water, waiting for her to take it. She put out her arms.

"Careful. It's heavy," he warned.

Cole was sitting too high and too far back on the bench to take the pan safely from him, so she slid forward. But at that instant, her towel snagged on the bench, came undone and fell in a heap around her. Panicking, Cole snatched the pan away from Blackfoot and succeeded only in sloshing water all over her exposed self. She looked down, stunned. Sure enough, there she was—in the buff, holding her pan of water as if it was some sort of ornamental bird bath. She looked up helplessly. "I'm sorry."

Adam's face was like a block of marble when he reached out to relieve her of the pan. "No need to apologize," he mumbled.

Cole made a valiant attempt to reclaim the pile of terry cloth around her, but her fingers felt like bread sticks and she was trembling all over.

"Don't cover yourself."

Cole glanced up; she must have heard wrong. "I beg your pardon?"

Adam's eyes slid over her body as she clutched the towel to her breasts. "I want to look at you," he said, holding out his hand.

What did he think she was: a nude model? She took his hand but the towel stayed in place as she stepped down to join him.

"I have a lot to apologize for," he said.

Cole's eyes widened in surprise. "No, you don't," she protested.

Adam shook his head. "I've behaved abominably, and none of it's your fault. I've led you on, I've hurt you and I've been denying things to myself that never should have been denied. I'm so sorry, Cole." His hand moved along her arm in a gentle caress.

Her eyes filled, his apology hurting almost as much as his rejection had. It was a different kind of pain, though, a bittersweet longing that tore at her, exposing the vital needs that she had denied in herself for so long.

Cole went into his arms, sighing, nearly overcome by the sense of security his embrace gave her. She knew she was strong and independent, but somehow in this man's arms, she didn't need to be. It felt good to let down her guard.

"Adam," she whispered, "you're so unreachable at times. Just when I think I'm getting to know you—"

"Shh, it's all right, darling," he said, his hand stroking the back of her neck. "Don't bother trying. My admirable qualities are so scarce they're not worth exploring. And having been alone for so long, I find it hard to open up with anyone."

Cole lifted her eyes to him. Being alone and unwilling to open up was something she could understand and she was about to tell him so, but the intensity of his emerald gaze was so overwhelming the words were left unspoken on her tongue. She had never seen a look so deep, so full of naked desire.

"The race we flew on the day I met you," he said huskily, "was the most difficult I'd ever flown, and it had nothing to do with the weather conditions."

"What was it then?" she murmured.

His arm tightened around her waist. "Having you so near, just the two of us alone, the rest of the world far below. You so beautiful, enchanting . . ."

A sympathetic chord resounded through Cole's fevered body. She had felt that way about him, blaming it on the thin air. Were the sparks between two people really such tangible things?

She lifted her arms from Adam's chest and wrapped them around his neck. "I felt the same way."

His mouth was so close to hers she could feel the gentle feathering of his breath on her lips. His eyes were green fire, devouring her upturned face. "I don't want to disappoint you, Cole.... You shouldn't expect too much from me."

She put her finger to his lips. "I'll take my chances."

With a low, anguished groan, Adam brought his mouth to Cole's and kissed her with savage, heart-numbing intensity. Hours, days, weeks of denial exploded into oblivion as they sought each other hungrily, greedily. Tongues tasted, lips caressed, teeth nipped and words of love were fed to each other in complete abandon.

Somehow the towels slipped away from their bodies and neither Cole nor Adam bothered to retrieve them; their usefulness was spent. Adam stepped back and drew in a sharp breath as his eyes consumed Cole's body. Only their fingers touched as she stood before him, naked, as trusting as a child but with the mature desires of a woman.

Adam's face was beaded with sweat, etched with yearning. So intense, so incandescent were his eyes they, rather than the cast-iron stove nearby, might have been the source of the room's fiery heat. "Shall we go back to the house?" he asked softly.

Cole shook her head. "Let's stay right here, please." The moment was too fragile, too long awaited, to risk shattering with relocation. Her lover understood; he bent down and spread the thick terry towels across the cedar floor.

Cole sank to her knees on the mat he'd prepared, her eyes never leaving his face. Adam picked up a dipper of water and threw it on the rocks. Steam rose with a soft hiss and clothed the room in velvet warmth. Within seconds, their bodies glistened anew.

Cole lay down, lifting her arms to him, and he came to her with soft whispers of her name, tenderly giving her the weight of his perfect body. As their flesh met, damp and slippery, ripples of ecstasy coursed through her; the sensation of touch, it seemed, had taken on new extremes in the hot, steamy room.

The silky hair on Adam's legs ignited Cole's thighs. His chest with its mat of dark curls tickled her breasts, deepening their hue as if with delicate brush strokes. His large, expressive hands stroked her face and wiped her brow gently.

After weeks of only imagining how Adam would feel, Cole set her hands free to explore him. His body was disciplined, hard and sinewy, his chest intractable, his buttocks firm but pliant as he moved his thigh between her legs. She felt the concave flex of his responding muscles and dug her fingers into the bristly juncture of his legs, gasping when his arousal met hers.

He claimed Cole's body with his tongue and lips, moving over her and giving her his undivided attention. Never had Cole been made to feel so beautiful, so completely a woman; nor had she known a lover could be so infinitely gentle and so completely a man. He took her in ways more intimate than she'd ever dared imagine, and each pleasure only exceeded the one before, until her whole body was writhing in need of him. She raised her hips and moved her body instinctively with the rhythm of his kisses. "Adam . . . please," she managed to gasp, her head thrown back and her breath ragged.

He slid up to meet her and, as he did so, entered her body, overwhelming her with the impact. She began to tremble and lose control. Digging her nails into his back, she was certain she would die from sheer pleasure. Adam wrapped his arms around her and kept their bodies still, letting her adjust to the feel of him inside her. "Hush, Cole," he whispered, calming her and bringing her to a high plateau from which their passion could be launched together.

He seemed to know exactly what to do. Cole could feel her dispersed emotions gather into the central core of her; she tightened around him, pulling and drawing him deeper as he began to stroke gently.

The cadence of their lovemaking commenced with hypnotic languor, but soon Adam became more commanding and masterful, taking Cole swiftly to new spheres of intensity. She clung to his broad back, wrapped her legs around him. Together, they rose, swelling and ebbing, soaring to a brilliant expanse where nothing existed beyond the moment.

When they could soar no higher, the stars exploded in white-hot radiance and the heavens roared and crashed, casting them ravaged and sated to a quiet shore beyond. Adam cried out Cole's name an instant after she'd gasped his. Then his head dropped to her shoulder and they lay still so the lingering entity of their union might be prolonged a moment or two longer.

Sometime later, as Cole lay on Adam's chest, her fingers idling in his curls, she marveled at how such a simple physical act could be so profound with the right person. And she no longer suffered any doubts—he was the right person.

As if in response, Adam opened his sleepy eyes and kissed the top of Cole's head. "I never would have believed it could happen," he murmured, "but I think I'm falling in love."

Cole lifted her head to look at him and, incongruously, an image of *Stargrazer* soaring off to some distant horizon flashed through her mind. The last thing she saw in Adam's eyes as he waved at her from the gondola was love.

7

THE INSTANT he saw Cole's face, Blackfoot cursed himself for having uttered such a misleading, irresponsible statement. But it was too late to fix things now. Her reaction might be understandably less than enthusiastic if he tried to explain that he hadn't meant those words quite the way they'd sounded.

He could read the expectation in her eyes as clearly as if she'd spoken aloud. *So you're falling in love with me—now what?* A legitimate question, but what was he supposed to say? I love you, Cole, but it doesn't mean we have a future together. In fact, we don't; there isn't a chance in a million.

Even a thick-skinned old reprobate like himself knew what a woman of Cole Jameson's caliber needed: comfort, security, a sense of belonging. She would need all of that and her independence besides, that singular quality of resilience that was uniquely Cole's. No one had the right to make her give it up. Hers was a tall order for a man to fill, but it was no more than she deserved. Too bad he was the last person in the world to be able to give her any of it.

Cole snuggled deeper into the crook of Blackfoot's arm; his spirits soared at the simple, loving gesture. "I have a confession to make, too," she said.

He stroked her hair with a large, rough palm. "What is it, love?"

"I peeked while you were undressing."

Blackfoot glanced down. She was smiling, but it was the kind of smile a person put on when they were saying something appropriate and not necessarily what they meant. Damn it, she was trying to let him off the hook. Now he felt guiltier than ever. Guilty, and something else . . . disappointed. Yeah, much as he hated to admit it, it would have been nice to hear her say she was falling in love with him, too.

No, that wouldn't have accomplished anything besides the stroking of his undeserving ego. Better to follow her lead and look on all this as a pleasant, casual encounter. And as long as he ended things today, that's all it would be: casual.

"It's okay," he admitted. "I took a peek or two myself."

"You beast!" Cole gave him a playful thwack on the chest. "How could you?"

"It couldn't have been simpler, or more rewarding." Blackfoot brought Cole to her feet and kissed the tip of her nose, carefully keeping his eyes averted to areas no lower than her throat. Otherwise, he feared they might not ever leave the steam room. "And now for a punishment befitting the crime."

"But you just admitted you're as guilty as I am!" Cole protested, laughing.

"Don't worry. I intend to take my fair share of the punishment. Come on, hurry up while you're still warm." He brought her outside, snatching up a couple of fresh towels on the way out. What this scenario needed right now, he decided, was a little less steam, and he broke into a loping run toward the lake, Cole's hand in his.

She was doing her best to pull in the opposite direction, but she was also laughing delightedly and was no match for his strength.

"You promised, no dips!" she cried out, her feet hitting the water an instant after his.

"I lied!" he tossed back with one final yank of her arm to wet her all over.

The lake was cool, refreshing, the water crystal clear, reflecting the surrounding circle of trees in a perfect mirror image. Blackfoot let go of her hand and was pleased to see her cast aside her inhibitions and adapt to her aquatic surroundings as if born to them. She dove underwater and moved through the depths with lithe grace. Her body was slender, delicate and so damned desirable it made his heart ache to watch her.

With a stab of outrage, he wondered how Cole's husband ever could have left her. He had to be some kind of a bastard, he thought, although Adam knew he wasn't exactly going to qualify for sainthood when he did the same thing.

He swam away from the shore, slicing through the water with powerful breaststrokes. He had to tell her everything. And it had to be now, while she could still dismiss him with a measure of dignity. It was tempting to let things go on for a while, pretend theirs was the same as any other budding relationship. But of course it wasn't. And if he waited, there was a good chance one of them—or both of them—would get in so deep there'd be no recovering.

He turned around and swam back until the water was shoulder level. "Cole, come here for a second."

As she swam toward him the evening sun rested on the lake's edge directly behind her, embellished by pastel clouds at either side. Adam cringed. Even Mother Nature was doing her best to make things difficult for him.

Cole stood up and combed back wet hair with her fingers. "What it it?" she asked, her smile radiant.

"I have something to tell you," he said, taking her hands in his.

Cole frowned slightly. "Sounds as if I'm not going to like this."

"Probaby not."

"Then don't say it!" she countered, pulling her hands away and closing them over his shoulders. "Not today, Adam, please. It's been such a perfect day. Don't spoil it."

Blackfoot curled his toes in the sandy lake bottom, trying to resist the feel of her silken, water-slick body rubbing against his, but it was a hopeless effort. She was right; this wasn't the time or the place, with both of them unclothed and happy. He had no right to ruin the moment for her . . . or for himself.

His hands slipped down to her gently rounded buttocks and he drew her closer. When Cole saw her protestations had won out, she lifted her mouth to his and kissed him. Her arms tugged his shoulders gently, urging him to relax and join her in an underwater swim. Between kisses, they took lungfuls of air and dove beneath the surface like a pair of sea creatures. Their arms entwined and their legs fluttering softly, they glided together along the bottom of the lake.

Cole's hair moved behind her like ebony ribbons and her lashes were long and spiky around her clear blue eyes. When she smiled, tiny bubbles emerged from her mouth and rose to the surface, which made him laugh, and bubbles of his own rose. When she reached out to ruffle his curls in aquatic slow motion, Blackfoot felt as though time had somehow ceased. For these brief fleeting moments, they could frolic in their primeval origins and never give a thought to the complications of the real world.

But time was running out and their lungs would tolerate no more of this delusion. Blackfoot brought Cole's face to his, tasting her wet lips and savoring the warmth of her mouth as they rose in tandem to the surface. They gasped for air together, and it seemed an especially intimate act, their mouths scant inches apart, sharing the same parcel of life-giving oxygen.

Treading water, Cole lifted her legs to wrap them around Adam; her breasts grazed tantalizingly across his chest. This time when their bodies came together, there was less urgency, and without words they responded to their resurgent passion. They took their time, savoring the subtle qualities of lovemaking they'd overlooked the first time.

He found every part of Cole enticing: the mildly salty tang of her skin, the firmness of her slender limbs, the soft bristliness at the core of her and he loved the way his hands fit around her bottom. When he entered her, he threw his head back in sheer unrestrained ecstasy. The sensation of Cole—of liquid satin—was over-

whelming . . . perfection. Their bodies were weightless
in the water and all of their energies seemed to flow like
molten lava from the rhythmic movements of their
union.

His arousal mounted swiftly, engulfing him as he
rode their escalating passion. The eruption, when it
burst through his body, was volcanic. Searing and undulating like streams of fire, untouched by the cool-
ness of the surrounding water. He felt Cole's responding
rhythms, her great, heaving sighs. He crushed her to
him; his heart hammered through his broad chest and
they succumbed to the fevered flow as one.

Then all was quiet. A timeless eternity later, they
drifted apart with only their fingers intertwined beneath the water's surface. Adam's eyes were calm and
replete, like jade pools, and they mirrored Cole's own
deep contentment. This time, no words were spoken;
there was no need. To put feelings into words would be
to glaringly understate what had transpired between
them.

Suddenly, it seemed, the sun disappeared and sur-
rendered the last of its warmth to the twilight air. Cole
began to shiver.

"Let's go back to the house," Adam said in a low
voice.

As they dressed in the sauna, Cole realized that ever
since they'd come out of the water she'd felt different
with Adam. Something even beyond their making love
had happened, something hard to name. A bond, at
once inseverable and fragile, had been created between them.

JAKE AND HESTER had gone to see a double feature at the movies, and there was a dinner of hickory-smoked ham left in the oven. After Cole and Adam finished eating, they went outside to sit on the steps of the front porch and sip their cognac. The air was still and the sky was like an inverted indigo bowl perforated by the glimmer of a million stars.

Darkness was kind to Adam's features. The shadows eased the crags of his face and outlined the firm structure of his cheekbones and jaw. The moonlight altered his eyes to two orbs of brilliant jet. He was leaning back with his elbows resting on the top step and his legs stretched out in front of him.

"I love the sounds of the country at night, don't you?" Cole asked, the profound silence between them making her nervous.

He turned to look at her. "Cole, we have to talk."

Something in the tone of his voice told Cole he wouldn't be put off any longer. "Fair enough," she said, wrapping her arms around her knees and drawing them up to her chin, "you talk, I'll listen."

"Do you remember when you asked me about being a doctor?"

Cole nodded. "You said you weren't practicing. I assumed your license was under suspension and you didn't like talking about it."

"You're half right. I don't like to talk about my profession to people who aren't involved with it, but I'm not under suspension. I'm a practicing surgeon and specialist in tropical diseases."

She swallowed hard. "Where?"

"Wherever the work takes me. South America next."

Cole drew in a deep breath. "Why have you waited so long to tell me?"

Adam ran his hands through his hair, and even in the tempering moonlight, his face was a study in anguish. "There are a thousand long and involved reasons, Cole. And at this moment, not one of them seems the least bit rational."

Gripping her crystal snifter tightly, Cole said, "Try me."

"All right . . . I've been practicing over fifteen years; first, in Ghana with the World Health Organization, I was involved with a program to eradicate yellow fever." He laughed, but it was a harsh, caustic laugh. "That would have been a simple job if we hadn't had to contend with malaria and river blindness and a hundred other endemic atrocities."

"It must have been a horrendous task," Cole acknowledged, feeling that even as he spoke, he was slipping away from her.

"By the time we finished our project, I was suffering from my first case of burnout and had to take nearly a year off before I could go back and face another assignment."

"I can appreciate that," said Cole.

He made a derisive sound. "Sure, if it only happens once, it's okay, but it happens to me almost more than I care to admit. I'm in the same situation now, just as I was four years ago, and just as I was three years before that. I reach a point where I can't take the fourteen-hour days, six days a week. I can't take the heat and the stench and the disease. I can't take any more children dying in my arms. . . ."

Adam was staring at Cole as he spoke, but he wasn't seeing her. By the tortured look in his eyes, Cole knew he was thousands of miles away. "No matter how hard I force myself to keep going," he went on, "there comes a time when my hands start to shake, my vision blurs and I know that if I see one more patient, my scalpel will slip . . ." Adam's voice cracked and he leaned forward, head in hands. "Thinking about it is torture enough, let alone talking about it."

Cole reached out and stroked the back of her hand along his arm. "But you're always been able to go back. That's the important thing."

"So far, but each time it gets harder and harder. And while I'm off ballooning or whatever the guilt is like a fist in my stomach."

"You shouldn't feel guilty. Everyone suffers from stress . . . I know I do."

Adam looked up with narrowed eyes, as if steeling himself against an inner pain. "Sure, but babies aren't dying because you're indulging your stress."

"You're not the only doctor out there," she reminded him in a soft but stern voice.

"I know, but there are never enough of us." He turned his head away, defeat implicit in his tone.

Cole rested her head on his shoulder and felt tension that hadn't been in him before. "When do you leave?" she asked.

"In early October, I hope, after the Jean Beauvais race. We have a team working in Ecuador, and one of them is taking a leave of absence in the fall. I have no choice but to take his place."

Cole squeezed her eyes shut. October...a scant three months away. He should've told her right away, but maybe he hadn't so he could— No, Adam wouldn't use her that way... of course he wouldn't!

Besides, he had tried to tell her earlier and she wouldn't let him. If he had taken advantage of the situation, well, so had she. There was no point in laying blame now.

She felt as though her heart was being torn out. If only it hadn't been so good between them, if only she didn't care—

"We might as well end things now, Cole, while we're still ..." The right word escaped him.

"Friendly?" Cole offered lamely.

"You could put it that way."

Cole took a large drink of cognac and lost herself for a moment in its pungent, fiery bouquet. Part of her wanted to scream and lash out at him for misleading her. Admittedly she'd allowed herself to be misled, and part of her wanted to squeeze every bit of happiness she could get from the next three months. But damn it, that was nothing more than an affair! A calculated season of terminal sex with nothing but a painful farewell to look forward to at the end of it all.

Perhaps Adam was right and it would be better to say goodbye right away. But Cole's emotional self rebelled at the thought. How could they end things now, when every day she would wake up and know that Adam was at Twin Elms or at his farm, a phone call away? There were some things beyond even the most disciplined of souls.

"If we could've just remained friends," said Adam, "we would have been able to keep in touch and get together every few years, the way Warren and I do." He gave a mirthless laugh. "At least, it sounded reasonable in theory."

"Mm, yes, but it doesn't work quite the same way for lovers, does it?" Cole took another sip of her drink, then turned to Adam. "I don't want to end it." She had an idea it was the false bravado of the dinner wine and brandy talking, but right now she didn't care who or what gave her the courage to say it, as long as it was said.

Adam looked unconvinced. "Why don't you take some time first to think about it before you decide?"

"No!" she countered emphatically. "I know what I'm getting myself into . . . and I can handle it."

He took her hand in his and traced her fingers one by one. "You'd only be shortchanging yourself, Cole. There's so little of me that I can share with you, and whatever you do get won't be worth a thing at the end. I don't want you to end up hating me." He looked up with an expression of searing concern.

"That won't happen!" Cole insisted, pivoting so she could face him squarely. "I know we only have until the race and I can accept it, I promise. We'll just take things one day at a time, and then . . . when the summer's over—" she lifted her hands and offered a brave smile "—we'll say so long."

He hesitated a long time before he spoke. "All right, Cole. If it's what you really want."

She nodded slowly. "It's what I really want."

8

ADAM MORE THAN MADE UP FOR his initial lack of enthusiasm during the weeks that followed. He spent every possible moment with Cole. They took in concerts, from Bach to Springsteen; they had old-fashioned picnics in the park; they went to museums and art galleries, the beach and the zoo; they stayed up late watching old movies and eating popcorn. They worked all hours on *Stargrazer II*. And they made love.

As the summer passed, they came to know each other's deepest and most intimate desires. No matter whether their mood was passionately romantic or whimsical or snuggly, their time together was never anything less than perfect.

By rights, Cole had no reason to feel sorry for herself; Adam was giving everything he could. He was kind, attentive, caring and sensitive to every nuance of her moods. But she wasn't adjusting to the limits of their relationship as well as she had hoped.

It wasn't that she doubted Adam's feelings. He seemed genuinely in love with her, and he told her so often. But if it bothered him to see the days fly by on the calendar, he didn't mention it. In the art of self-discipline, he made Cole look like a rank amateur.

No matter how much she tried to rationalize things, Cole's feelings had developed a mind and will of their own. Her love for Adam had outgrown their allotted measure of time and was spilling over into the future where it had no place. She was compelled to demand more than cloudless days and laughter.

In a matter of weeks, Blackfoot would leave her forever to resume the life of Dr. Adam Torrie, and Cole ached to be a part of that world, too. She wanted to be there waiting for him at the end of the day to kiss away the hurt, to massage the stress and the fatigue from his broad shoulders. She wanted the opportunity to make Adam happy when he needed it most.

There were times—and they'd become more frequent of late—when she found herself imagining that Adam wanted her there with him, too. They'd be having a wonderful conversation and suddenly it would lag, the silence prickling with unspoken sentiments. She had the distinct impression he wanted to ask her something but didn't know how, or didn't dare. Cole would hold her breath, anticipating, but then the moment would pass and he would launch into some safe and neutral topic.

Somehow, there never was a right time or place for Cole to bring the matter up. Either the words wouldn't come, or they were forgotten in the events of the moment. She couldn't bring herself to jeopardize one single minute of the time they had, and perhaps Adam wanted to keep things that way, too. Still, Cole had an idea there was still one perfect opportunity for her and Adam to face the future honestly and openly. She needed only to have Warren's cooperation.

She brought it up with Warren during lunch. The restaurant, with its blue-tiled walls and potted plants, was, as usual, packed with the business luncheon crowd. Cole had finished her Spanish omelet and was waiting for coffee to arrive; Warren had ordered carrot cake.

"I have to talk to you about Adam," Cole began.

"You two having problems?" he asked. Cole couldn't help but notice Warren didn't look surprised.

"Not exactly—"

"Warren! Long time no see!" An outrageously curvaceous blonde stopped at their table to display her prominent assets.

Warren's eyes shifted helplessly from one woman to another, finally succumbing to Cole's vituperative glare. He knew what had to be done. "Sheila, hello. Nice to see you," he gushed. "But would you excuse us? I've just proposed to this lady here, and she hasn't given me her answer yet."

Sheila turned to issue Cole a look oozing with venom, which Cole promptly returned with a guileless look of her own. It was a ploy they'd had to resort to on more than one occasion, she and Warren. It was the price one paid for going to public places with the local heartthrob. Sheila finally sashayed back to her own table with hardly a whimper. The damage was never permanent. Warren could call Sheila later, grief-stricken, and tell her his proposal had been turned down. In no time, he'd be on his way to an evening of rapturous commiserations.

He returned his attention to Cole. "You were saying?"

She paused until their waiter finished serving the coffee and dessert. "I'm not sure how to say this without sounding like the worst kind of manipulator.... I'd like Adam and me to grow closer ... and I think I've come up with a way to do that." She waved her fingers through the air. "Not that I really have to do anything, I mean . . ." Oh, hell, this was coming out badly!

Warren chewed his carrot cake and regarded her thoughtfully. "I had the impression the two of you couldn't be happier."

"That's true," she insisted with a tinge of forced exuberance, "but ... well, it can't be real happiness when there's this inevitable end looming up ahead! I mean, it's not genuine happiness, is it? It's—I don't know, an alternate way to expend nervous energy or something."

Her handsome friend—the wretch—burst out laughing at Cole's lame description. When Cole failed to join in the levity, he mustered up his composure. "Hope you'll pardon me for begging the obvious, but didn't the two of you already agree on the terms of your . . . relationship, given Blackfoot's priorities?"

Her spoon continued to make unnecessary circuits around the coffee cup. "Yes."

"And do you realize that his profession is not one he can simply transplant to Philadelphia, even for you?"

"I know that, too."

Warren sat back and eyed her suspiciously. "Listen, gorgeous, I've got this funny feeling I know what you're driving at, and I don't like the sound of it. You can't just give up all of your commitments here and sail off to—"

"Nobody said anything about giving up commitments!" Cole protested. "Not yet, anyway."

"Good, 'cause if you're looking for someone to commend you, you've come to the wrong guy." He pointed a warning finger. "And don't expect me to talk to Blackfoot on your behalf, either. He'll just tell me to mind my own damned business, and he'd be right. I've interfered enough already."

Cole pursed her lips and decided not to remind Warren of how many times she had willingly stepped in to get him out of some predicament with a woman. It had nothing to do with the issue at hand.

"I have a favor to ask you, but you don't have to talk to Blackfoot," she said. "What I'd like is to take your place in the Jean Beauvais race."

For the first time since she'd known him, Warren was completely taken aback. In this instance, she didn't blame him. He and Blackfoot had worked long and hard to prepare for the competition, and she was asking a great deal of him to give it up. Perhaps even too much, she admitted as she watched his expression.

"You want to copilot?" he asked.

Cole nodded.

"It's a forty-eight-hour race. Do you realize how grueling that is?"

"I do. That's why I intend to take plenty of practice flights and get my pilot's license before the summer is over."

Warren scratched his chin. He still looked as though he'd just had the breath knocked out of him. "I suppose it's none of my business why you think this'll make any difference."

Cole made a noncommittal gesture that she hoped conveyed a sense of supreme self-confidence. "You'll find out eventually."

"Does Blackfoot know about this yet?" Warren asked.

"Good heavens, no!" she replied, and wished she hadn't sounded quite so appalled. It wasn't as though she was afraid to face him or anything.

"All right, Cole, if it means that much to you—and it must, or you never would have asked—" he took a sip of his coffee and his eyes never left her face "—I'll let you take my place, on one condition."

She drew in a quick breath. "Name it."

"I want you to promise me you'll tell Blackfoot about this right away."

"What makes you think I wouldn't?" she asked, blanching slightly.

"I wasn't implying that you wouldn't, but I get the feeling you're not really sure you're doing the right thing. It would probably be tempting to let Blackfoot think nothing has changed. But this competition is the most important one he's ever flown—it's important to all of us—and I won't let you spring anything on him at the last minute."

Of course, Warren was right. Cole remembered what Adam had said once about the perils of flying on negative emotions. She'd never forgive herself if something were to happen on her account. "I'll tell him today," she said. "I'm going to the farm right after work."

"Good. There's just one more thing. Blackfoot is still the pilot, and he has the last official word. If he doesn't go along with this, there's nothing either of us can do."

Cole's fingers tightened around the coffee cup. "I know that. Do you think there's a chance he might not go along with it?"

Warren gave her a sad smile and reached across the table for her hand. "Sweetheart, if Blackfoot turns you down, then he's a crazier damned fool than I am for letting you go."

HESTER SIMS was in the front yard digging up a flower bed when Cole pulled into the driveway of the farmhouse. The older woman got up to greet her, pulling work gloves from her hands and brushing the dirt from her overalls.

"How are you, Cole? Didn't think we'd get to see you until the weekend. Is everything all right?"

"Everything's fine." Cole gave her a fond hug. "Guess I just can't keep myself away from this place. Your flowers look fabulous, Hester. You've got the greenest thumb of anybody I know."

The two of them strolled along the flagstone path past rainbow clusters of impatiens, profusions of honeysuckle and yellow climbing roses. "I've always loved flowers," Hester said. "They don't sass and they make a body feel good just by bein' themselves."

Cole laughed gently despite the knot of grinding nerves in her stomach. "We could all learn a thing or two from them, couldn't we? Is Adam home?"

"He's right where you'll always find him these days."

"The barn?"

"The barn." Hester sent Cole off with an encouraging nudge. "Now be sure to come up to the house later on for some coffee. I baked cinnamon rolls fresh this afternoon."

"I'd love to." If I'm still welcome around here, Cole added silently.

The windows and the large double doors of the barn were open wide to take advantage of the last rays of sunlight. Cole could see Adam inside working and she stopped a short distance from the door to watch him.

Kneeling in front of the gondola, he was sanding its surface with smooth, diligent strokes. It made Cole smile to watch him work. She didn't know too many men who would bother to tackle such a formidable project for one race. And it was a task that would go unnoticed by the rest of the world. This sense of discipline was one of the qualities she loved most about Adam. When something was important to him, he saw it through with quiet strength. Even though...

Cole wrapped her arms around her midriff and refused to let herself dwell on negative reflections. There were times, blue days, when she felt as though Adam had her boxed in an airtight compartment with a one-way door; there was no room to stretch or grow. His attitude relayed the unspoken message that Cole could either live—and love—within the confines he'd laid out or she could leave, knowing she'd never be allowed back in again.

Just when she'd be all set to lambast him, he'd do something crazy and sweet, like fix her a bubble bath by candlelight, with champagne chilling nearby. Then she'd realize she had no basis for her feelings. He was doing everything he'd promised to do; her insecurities were not his fault.

Moreover, Cole reminded herself, she was here to convince him how wonderful it would be to spend a week together in France, the country of love. It would hardly help to arrive with a big fat chip on her shoulder.

Cole squeezed her eyes shut and pressed icy fingers to her temples. Then, fastening a determined smile on her face, she snuck up behind Adam, knelt down and covered his eyes with her hands. "Guess who?" she said.

He stiffened for an instant then dropped the sandpaper to take Cole's hands and kiss her palms. "I give up. Which of my many admirers are you?"

Cole gave him a playful boot in the rear with her knee. "You beast. You're getting to be worse than Warren."

Swiveling around on the balls of his feet, Blackfoot rewarded her with a generous smile. "Thanks for the compliment, but I'll never hold a candle to Warren. To what do I owe this pleasant surprise?"

"Oh, just lucky, I guess." Cole moved closer for his kiss. "Sure you don't mind some company?"

"Are you kidding? You are the most exciting thing that's happened to me all day. If I never see another piece of sandpaper in my life, it'll be too soon." He brought her to her feet and his fingers lingered in her hair. Then he turned and made a broad sweeping gesture with his arm. "So what do you think of the gondola so far?"

Cole pushed back her reasons for being here and looked over Adam's handiwork. She had to admit the man was a true artisan. "It's beautiful and so sleek; it looks just like a boat. Do you actually anticipate having to land in water?"

"Hope not, but if the choice comes down to landing in a lake or the Matterhorn, I'll go for the lake. At least I'll have the option."

The silence stretched a little too long between them.

"Uh...what's this little sectioned-off area for?" Cole asked hastily.

"The portable john."

"Oh." She chuckled. "Well, I'm sure the folks down below will appreciate your forethought."

Adam folded his arms and gave Cole a curious look. "Correct me if I'm wrong, but I have the feeling this visit of yours isn't entirely spontaneous."

Cole turned to look at his craggy features and couldn't decide whether to blurt out everything or forget the whole idea. "Do you?" she asked in a small voice.

He steered her to a bench and sat her down. "Tell me, Cole; what's bothering you?"

Cole laced her fingers together, unlaced them and laced them again. "Warren and I were talking, and . . ." No, that sounded too conspiratorial, and Warren had nothing to do with any of this. She tried again. "I-asked-Warren-if-I-could-fly-in-his-place-in-the-race-and-he-said-I-could." She clamped her mouth shut and waited for Adam to explode.

He didn't. "Why did you do that?" he asked, sounding genuinely puzzled.

Cole exhaled for what seemed like forever. "Because . . . I thought the two of us—that is, you and I—

might benefit from some time away together...just the two of us." She'd already decided the second half of her plan would wait until they were in France.

Up until now, they had been sitting closely enough that Adam's denim-covered thigh and Cole's white-cotton-covered thigh were touching. He moved away slightly, only enough for all physical contact to be removed, but to Cole the gesture seemed as blatant as a scream, the distance between them, leagues.

"I wasn't aware that you and I were suffering from a lack of closeness or privacy. We're together all the time." Adam gave her a probing look. "What more do you want, Cole?"

"What more do I want?" she returned, in a tone several notes shriller than normal. "There's no future for us, so I'd just like to extend the present if I can. Besides, I've never had a chance to share one of your adventures, the way Warren has, and I'd really love to do that . . . once." Cole could hardly believe what she was hearing herself say. She was deliberately leading him down the wrong path, lying about why she wanted to fly with him. This was idiotic; she'd never be able to convince him of her sincerity to share his life after today. Perhaps she ought to tell him everything right now. "I'm not asking too much, am I?" said her mutineering voice.

Adam placed large square palms on his thighs and stood up. Then he began to pace the width of the barn. "No," he said, "you're not asking too much. But I hope you won't be too disappointed when I refuse your offer."

Cole felt walls closing in on her. "Wh-why won't you let me fly with you?" she stammered.

Adam didn't answer right away. "Well, for one thing, the Jean Beauvais race is one of the most difficult of all flying competitions. It's nothing like the romantic countryside floats you're used to."

"Romantic floats?" Cole repeated, sitting up straight. "Since when were rotors and wind shears and storms ingredients of a romantic float?"

For a fleeting instant their eyes touched and Cole would have sworn there was a glimmer of understanding in the green depths of Adam's eyes, as if he somehow knew what her ultimate intentions were. But it was only a glimmer.

"It takes a lot more than being a knowledgeable balloonist," he replied, "which I admit you are. It also takes a great deal of stamina to endure forty-eight hours aloft. I can't risk having you collapse from exhaustion halfway through the race."

The walls were getting closer.

"I'm not lacking in stamina!" Cole protested. "When I'm excited or under pressure I hardly need any sleep at all. I haven't had so much as a cold in ten years, and the only time I've ever missed work is when I sprained my ankle in a balloon landing! So why on earth would I turn into some dizzy, fainting petticoat for one race?" She was feeling the constriction more strongly than ever, and her rebuttals seemed to be landing way off their mark. Cole's hopes were sinking fast.

"I'm sorry, Cole. My mind is made up. I don't see that any good can come of our prolonging this relationship past the end of summer. We'd both be suffering from a lot of emotional stress during the race, and you know how dangerous that can be." His fists were jammed into the pockets of his jeans, but Cole no longer found the gesture so endearing. "I'd rather remember us the way we were, here at home. If Warren doesn't want to co-pilot, I'll get one of my ground crew in France to fill in."

Cole dug her fingers into the bench. He hadn't even given her suggestion a fighting chance, as though he'd already prepared himself in advance for her argu-ments. It suddenly dawned on her that she'd never really held a place in Adam's life, any more than she had a place aboard *Stargrazer*. She'd been a stopgap, a pleasant way to alleviate the tedium between gluing the balloon and planing the gondola. All this rubbish about love—it was just words!

When Cole spoke, her tone was deliberately aloof. "I think, after all this time, I've finally gotten the mes-sage."

Adam's expression grew defensive, as she'd expected it would. "What's that supposed to mean?"

"It's not my safety or anyone else's that you're think-ing about, is it?"

"Yes, it—"

"Oh, for God's sake, stop being so patronizing for once!" Cole got to her feet, her instinct for survival taking over where love had fallen short. "I've been de-luding myself all this time, thinking you cared, but now I know—"

"Cole, you're wrong. I do care."

She was past the point of listening; no one was going to imprison her emotions again. Her eyes were blue ice and her hands were clenched into slender fists at her sides. "Sure, you care. For the requisite amount of time, you care. The same way as if you were riding white-water rapids, you care about keeping your raft afloat! Then when the ride is over, you can forget about it and go on to the next little adventure!"

Adam's look of sympathy was altering to one of anger, but Cole stood her ground.

"You use all of your love when you're being the good doctor," Cole went on to say, "but when the time comes for you to be Blackfoot again, that's it for sentimentality, isn't it?"

"Cole, shut up!" He made a move toward her.

She took a sideways step and her chin began to quiver. Damn it, not that! The worst, the very worst thing she could do now was get...sentimental. "I tried," she said in a strictly measured tone, "I honestly tried to live up to the terms of our...agreement, but I can't function that way. I can't do things just for the sake of doing them, with no purpose." She backed her way to the door and gripped the aged door frame with one hand, pointing at Adam with the other. "Someday, when you're being Blackfoot and not Dr. Torrie, you're going to...oh, hell, I don't know...climb a mountain, and you're going to discover it doesn't give you the same old thrill that it used to. Worse, once you've realized it, you'll have to climb back down and find out you're all alone in the world. That's when you're going to miss me, Adam! That's when you're going to realize the love of a good woman is worth a dozen Everests!" Cole flicked away a tear. "And that's too bad, because I don't intend to sit around and wait for you to figure it out!" She pivoted sharply on one heel and walked out the door.

For one brief instant, she saw his face. Anger had been replaced by an expression of raw pain. But Cole couldn't allow a display of remorse to topple her new-found conviction. She urged her unwilling legs to continue walking.

"Go ahead, Cole," Adam called out in his deep, husky voice. "Leave me if you want to, but I do love you—I always will."

She stopped dead in her tracks, Adam's pronouncement colliding against her with the force of a brick wall. Then she shook her head firmly. He was only playing his trump card, hoping to buy himself enough time to finish out the summer with her. It wasn't going to work, though she couldn't stop herself from whispering, "I love you, too."

Only a robin or two heard.

WARREN TRACKED Blackfoot down at Twin Elms the next day. He was hunched over a medical journal at the small table in his gazebo. A plate of fish and chips, barely touched, sat off to the side.

Blackfoot looked up when his friend walked in. "How ya doin, Sanders?" He smiled, oblivious to the fact that Warren hadn't knocked. They'd been informal with each other in the dorm years ago, and neither of them considered the passage of time sufficient reason to alter old habits.

Ignoring the greeting, Warren pointed a finger at the curly-haired man. "Look here, Blackfoot, I've put up with a lot from you over the years. Missed appointments, last-minute cancellations for no good reason, bullheadedness, but I've never known you to be such an unthinking, insensitive, shortsighted jerk! Are you vying for martyrdom, or are you just plain stupid?"

Blackfoot's smile faded. "What the hell are you talking about?"

"I'm talking about you turning down Cole's offer to copilot for you in France!"

"Oh, that." Blackfoot closed the journal and pushed it aside, along with his uneaten dinner. "She told you, did she?"

"No, she did not tell me. I had to drag it out of her. After you sent her away, she spent the whole evening alone at home with the phone unplugged. I thought she was with you until I saw how she looked this morning." Warren's rage deflated and he sank into a chair across from his friend. "Jeez, buddy, what were you thinking, turning down an offer like that from a woman like her?"

"First of all, I didn't send her away; she left. Secondly, I'm not sure it's a good idea for us to be discussing a woman we both obviously care about." When Warren flinched, Blackfoot felt a respondent tug in his own heart. The poor guy, he had it bad. They both did.

Warren jumped up from his chair and went to the small fridge for a beer, another long-accepted custom. "Yeah, we both care for her, but I cared enough to give her up. I didn't expect you to do the same thing after all I did for you." Warren stopped, bottle opener in one hand, beer in the other. He hadn't meant for that to slip out.

"And what exactly did you do?" Blackfoot's voice was guarded.

The blond man turned around to level blue-gray eyes at his friend. "I pretended to injure my back so the two of you could meet. I lied to Cole about you so she'd get a chance to like you before she found out what kind of life you lead. I gave you guys an opportunity to hit it off together, and you blew it!"

Blackfoot groaned, lowering his craggy face into his hands and rubbing his forehead. "I oughta kill you, Warren." Then he looked up. "But I guess I won't. I know how much flying that elimination race meant to you, and to give up the Jean Beauvais, too. That's some sacrifice, even if it is misguided."

"You've got it wrong. Flying the Jean Beauvais race was strictly Cole's idea, and believe me, it wasn't easy not to turn her down. Especially knowing it wasn't going to make things any better between the two of you, like she was hoping it would. You'd still be the same bullheaded pariah you always were, and kiss her off at the end of the race."

"If you knew all that, why'd you bother setting us up in the first place? Cole's one terrific lady, and I...I care for her a lot, but as for a future? Forget it!"

"Why?" demanded Warren. "Why the bloody hell should you forget it? Even though both of you would rather choke than admit it, she's crazy about you, too."

"And what am I supposed to do about it, Sanders? In a few weeks I'm going to Ecuador, for who knows how long. Then probably Indonesia after that, and after that I don't know. Does everyone expect me to come right out and ask the woman to give up her designer clothes, her condominium, her classy advertising job to be a doctor's wife in the middle of a jungle?" *Wife?* Blackfoot swallowed hard.

"I don't see why you can't," his friend answered in quiet challenge.

Blackfoot snatched his beer from Warren. "No damn way!"

"What's the matter? Afraid she might take you up on it?"

"No! Yes—I mean . . ." Blackfoot sighed deeply and tasted the ale. "Look, I've been this route before, trying to fit a woman into my life. And Atalaya would have been perfect. She was a nurse; she worked beside me. She understood the life, the long hours, the primitive surroundings. She didn't mind my coming home with bloodstains on my shirt. She could discuss schistosomiasis or the side effects of quinine—"

Warren slammed his drink on the table. "Yeah, sure, Torrie. You two might have lived in constant blissful misery, talking disease and medicine twenty-four hours a day. Nice life. And Atalaya's been dead for eight years, Blackfoot. It's about time you stopped waiting for her clone to appear!"

"I'm not!" growled Blackfoot, seething with the knowledge that Warren might be half right. At least, until he had met another black-haired woman, one with eyes as blue as the sky. "Cole is not Atalaya's clone. Cole Jameson is special. She's . . . she's not like anyone else I've ever met."

"Okay, so why don't you just let her fly the race with you?" said Warren. "I know it'd mean a lot to her."

Blackfoot shook his head. "What's the use? I can't even figure out what she sees in me. No, Warren, she's better off without me. The sooner, the better."

Warren didn't answer right away. Then he took one last drink and set the half-full bottle down. "Okay, buddy, it's your life." He headed toward the door.

"Warren?"

He stopped. "Yeah?"

"Have you told Cole what you did, faking your injury?"

"No," Warren said quietly, turning to face the friend who was even lonelier than he was. "I didn't tell Cole . . . and if anyone ever does, I'll call him a liar."

9

THEY WERE CALLING IT the hottest August on record. For over three weeks, the temperatures had smoldered relentlessly in the upper nineties, the humidity so oppressive that Philadelphia's entire population seemed imbued with permanent scowls.

Cole, after a particularly trying day at work, staggered into her living room and flopped down on the couch, every vestige of her salesmanlike enthusiasm long since depleted. Clutching a stack of mail like a makeshift fan, she directed the breeze toward her neck and sighed.

"Aaah...that's better," she said aloud, closing her eyes gratefully in a state approaching bliss. If this inferno kept up much longer, she was going to have to seriously consider installing air-conditioning in her car.

Sitting up, Cole riffled through the mail, a few bills and the rest third class. Didn't anyone write letters anymore? Peeling open the electric bill with one coral-frosted nail, she nearly swooned when she read the amount. So much for car improvements, she thought, and sailed the offending bit of paper impulsively across the room. Her budget was being ravaged just to keep this condominium air-conditioned.

Cole dropped the rest of the unopened mail beside her when a postcard fell out from between the envelopes labeled "Occupant." "What's this?" She picked it up and examined the scenic view of Mount Rainier. "I don't know anyone in Washington." She turned it over and scanned the handwriting.

You were right. I climbed 14,000 feet and it didn't do a thing for me. Wanted to try Everest, but it's booked solid for six years. I'm coming home next week. We need to talk. Please hold your fire until I've had five minutes of your time.

Adam

Like a toy train, Cole's eyes rode over and over the tracks of Adam's cryptic message until the words were engraved on her mind. She let the postcard flutter to her lap.

Adam Torrie.

She hadn't uttered the name in six weeks. Not that he hadn't been on her mind; in fact, quite the opposite was true. It seemed no matter what Cole saw or read or did, she would find herself trying to imagine Adam's opinion and reaction to a situation. In the short time they'd been together, she had all too easily accustomed herself to sharing her life with that man. Damn it, anyway! Why did he have to come around and mess everything up again?

It should have been a relatively simple matter to put that particular episode of her life behind her. After all, the man had frustrated and infuriated her no end, at times. In Cole's herculean efforts to forget him, she had started a rigorous weight-training program and joined a squash ladder, where she was quickly gaining a reputation for playing killer games. In addition, she was seriously considering a career change. She was still young enough, mobile, and it would do her good to relocate where there were no familiar places and no memories. Where she was going and what she would do, she hadn't the foggiest; but somehow the mere contemplation of a change helped.

Cole knew now how badly she'd handled things with Adam; or perhaps manipulated was a better word for it. The wisdom of hindsight told her they might have had a chance if only she'd let things take their course instead of twisting them to her advantage. Instead of backing him against the wall, how much nicer it would have been to hear Adam admit of his own accord that he couldn't bear to leave her. And even though he hadn't, she'd learned a lot from Adam about herself, about people . . . about love. Too bad she'd learned it too late.

CHOPIN WAS HAVING an off day. His cello sonata in G minor was not weaving its usual magic. Cole tossed the stereo a reproving look and checked her watch for the eighteenth time. Technically, Adam was due in five minutes, but she'd gotten ready three hours early, just in case his timing was still bad.

She stood up and went to the hall mirror for another merciless self-critique. After peering closely, Cole decided that with any luck, there was a good half hour remaining before discernible—and irreversible—wilt set in. Cool detachment during a heat wave was a near impossible state to maintain for long.

For the first time in Cole's brief history with Adam Torrie, the door bell rang at precisely the expected hour, which for some reason rattled her far more than tardiness would have. Walking on legs that had been forewarned not to buckle, Cole went to the door and swung it open. One glance at the man was enough for the last of her composure to burst like a bubble.

Over the past few days, Cole had thoroughly convinced herself that Adam would arrive at her door looking haggard, drawn or at least a trifle penitent. But damn it all, he looked fabulous! Wearing a shirt of unbleached cotton and brown chino pants, he seemed darker, healthier and more self-assured than Cole had ever seen him.

"Hello, Cole."

"Hello, Adam. Come in." Cole stepped back and motioned him inside. As she closed the door, she could feel his eyes moving over her body as if in reminiscence. It was much too hot to court formality, so she was wearing a velour shorts set in a deep shade of violet trimmed with white. Funny how five minutes ago, the outfit hadn't seemed nearly so short, nor so tight.

"What have you done to yourself?" Adam asked with his usual rough candor.

Cole did her best to sound desperate. "Wh-why? What do you mean?"

"I used to think your body was perfect, but you seem to have managed to improve on it somehow."

Ripples of pure pleasure ran up and down Cole's newly toned body and she smiled. "I've been trying to work on my stamina." Her expression not entirely guileless, Cole led him into the living room and invited him to sit down. Surreptitiously, she glanced at her watch. Five minutes, starting . . . now.

"Chopin?" Adam asked, cocking his ear toward the music.

"Yes, it is. I find him soothing sometimes." She strode purposefully to the stereo and turned it off. Mood music was not particularly appropriate right now.

Adam settled himself quite nicely on the sofa while Cole backed into a chair a safe distance away. Suddenly, much to her dismay, she could not decide what to do with her hands. At such a moment as this, Marlene Dietrich would have picked up a cigarette, inserted it into a gold-tipped holder and watched with feline amusement while her hapless suitor lunged across the room to light it. Lacking such props, Cole weaved her fingers together and jammed them into her lap.

"So . . . what have you been up to these past few weeks, besides mountain climbing?" As she spoke, her eyes drifted down to Adam's loose-fitting shirt, which still managed to emphasize the hard contours of his torso underneath. Rattled, Cole wondered if it was necessary for him to leave the top three buttons undone like that.

"Do you really want to know, or do you just want me to respond with an appropriate 'not much'?"

Oh, Adam, must you always be so unflinchingly blunt? A person should not have to admit to a preference for clichés over an honest answer. In this case, however, she would have gladly settled for the anonymous niceties of chitchat.

He sat back and stretched out his arms along the back of the couch, looking very pleased with himself. "I did something I've wanted to do for years. I bought a motorbike and drove across the country. Cole, you would not believe how fabulous people are right here in the good old U.S. of A."

So wanderlust had struck again. Cole tried to zero in on the unpleasant feeling in the pit of her stomach and was shocked to discover it was not a judgmental response, but a most definite case of jealousy. "How nice," she replied. "Mount Rainier, I take it, was the end of your journey?"

Adam nodded. "By the time I hit the west coast, I'd had enough of being saddle sore. I sold the bike, climbed the mountain and flew home."

Cole crossed her legs and folded her hands over one knee. "I see. That's certainly an interesting way to see America." Inwardly, Cole cringed at her pointed lack of enthusiasm. She didn't mean for her words to come out sounding that way, nor was she deliberately flaring her nostrils. They were, unfortunately, doing that all by themselves.

Her guest was far from offended. He seemed to be trying his best to suppress a grin. "I didn't exactly make the trip to please my grade-five geography teacher."

"Oh?" She'd sooner choke than inquire why he did it, and she told him so with her eyes.

"I did it to try and get you out of my mind," he offered, unbidden.

By some cruel trick of fate, Cole swallowed the wrong way and began to choke. She sat up straight and pounded her chest with an open hand. It served her right for being churlish.

"Were you—" Cole paused to clear her throat "—er, successful?"

"Do you think I'd be here if I had been?"

She looked at him askance. "I guess not. So why are you here?"

Running his fingers through auburn curls, Adam displayed the first sign of uncertainty since he'd arrived. "Two reasons. First, I want to apologize."

Cole shrank in her seat, waiting for the inevitable sensation of panic to flood over her. But strangely enough, it didn't come. The last thing in the world she would have expected to feel, sitting here with Adam, was comfortable.

"You have nothing to apologize for," she said, meaning it.

He shook his head. "I should never have let you get involved with me. I fully expected you to reach your breaking point before the summer was over, but I went ahead and used you anyway."

Moving her hand along the armrest of her wicker chair, Cole was surprised to note her fingers were trembling only slightly. Adam's confession should have enraged her, or at the very least offended her. Why on earth was she reacting as though it was the kindest thing he'd ever said? Had she really grown up so much in these past few weeks . . . or had she simply stopped caring?

Cole looked up with steady blue eyes. "If my memory serves me correctly, no one had to twist my arm to become your lover. I'm certainly old enough to take responsibility for the things I do, including making mistakes."

"But you deserve to settle down, share a home with someone."

"I used to think so," she answered, smiling wistfully, "but I've done a lot of thinking about that lately. It's true, I like to feel secure; I like to know where I'm headed. But somehow the thought of a house in the suburbs with three kids and a station wagon terrifies me. I've developed this fear of becoming . . . boring. I guess I have you to thank for that."

Adam gave a kind laugh. "I'm not sure it's something I should be thanked for. But if suburban life isn't what's right for Cole Jameson . . . what is?"

She was hoping he wouldn't ask, since it was the one area she hadn't worked out to her satisfaction yet. "I don't know," she finally admitted, "but right now, I'm working hard and trying a lot of things I've never done before. When I find what it is that makes me happy, I'll know."

Adam leaned forward and rested his elbows on his knees. "And I'm sure you'll find it someday, Cole. You deserve to be happy." Though he was too far away to touch her, his gentle gaze seemed to reach out in tacit understanding. "Will you let an old friend know when it happens?"

Something in his words shredded her heart to ribbons; perhaps it was the way he had said *friend*. In Cole's unrelenting mind, the word came out sounding like . . . *lover*. But that was all in the past, there was nothing to resurrect.

"Yes," she answered quietly, "I'll let you know when it happens."

Seeing him again, here in the comfort of her living room, Cole realized how much she had missed him. She'd missed his laugh, his earthy sense of humor, his unapologetic love for life, all of the very special elements that comprised Blackfoot, alias Dr. Adam Torrie. If she were to cast away all of those fine and rare qualities simply because she'd once imagined herself in love with the man, she'd be hurting nobody but herself. She was lucky to have Warren as one of her friends; how much luckier she would be if she could count Adam among them, too.

"You said you had two reasons for coming here," she reminded him, having completely forgotten about the five-minute limit.

"I have," he said. "I'd like you to be my copilot for the Jean Beauvais race in France."

Cole blinked and shook her head. "I'm not sure I heard you correctly."

"You heard me, all right," Adam assured her, "but I can appreciate your reluctance to believe it."

"What's the matter? Did your ground crew quit?"

Blackfoot laughed at Cole's frankly suspicious expression. "No, no, they didn't quit."

"And what about Warren?"

"At the moment, Warren is my second choice, after you."

This was too easy and much too unexpected. There had to be a catch. "Why the sudden change of heart?" asked Cole.

Adam shifted in his seat, crossing one leg over the other. He looked quite sincere, all things considered. "It wasn't that sudden, really. While I was on the road

I thought a lot about what you said when...the last time we saw each other, about wanting to share my adventures. I guess I was treating you like a woman instead of a first-class aeronaut. I know one race can't make up for everything I put you through, but . . . maybe you'll get some enjoyment out of it."

Cole lifted a sly brow. "But what if I faint . . . or pull the wrong cord? And what about negative emotions?"

"I'm willing to take my chances."

Her face lit up with a grin of sheer delight. No one could be more anxious than she to chart a new course with Adam. But this time, she would not be so foolish as to look beyond the race . . . or to look beyond their friendship. "I'd be thrilled to copilot for you, Adam," Cole said, her blue eyes sparkling.

10

THE PARISIAN CABBIE'S beady eyes seemed to leap right out from the rearview mirror every time Cole's gaze swiveled past him. Ignoring him did no good, nor was staring ice-blue daggers a deterrent; both methods merely fueled his lusty ogling. Quite apart from her annoyance at being assessed like a slab of meat, Cole would have preferred that he direct his attention to the traffic now and again. Ever since leaving the airport, the driver seemed determined to hurtle his fare through the city at cataclysmic speeds, barely missing pedestrians and careening around monuments erected in the middle of intersections as though maneuvering through some giant slalom course.

Adam burst out laughing when Cole slammed into his side at another two-wheeled corner. "Aren't you enjoying your adventure?"

Cole swore indelicately when her purse slid onto the floor again. "That's not funny. We should have flown in on *Stargrazer*."

"I'm sorry, Cole." He put an arm around her tense shoulder, if only to ease her around the cabbie's maniacal corners. "I didn't mean to laugh. I've just never seen you quite so unglued before, a seasoned solo balloonist yet."

Cole gave him a baleful look. "I've had my pilot's license for all of eight days, and besides, the skies will never be as treacherous as . . . this!" She pointed at the bedlam that was Paris, then realized the sights were becoming increasingly familiar to her. "Adam, look!" she cried, terror forgotten for the moment. "We're going over the Seine! There's the Left Bank, the Right Bank . . . and over there the Eiffel Tower!"

He leaned across her for a better view. "Sure enough," he quipped. "We must be in the right city."

For a brief instant, the glory of Paris faded beside the presence of crisp auburn curls, a rugged and weathered neck and the tingly male scent of Adam mere inches from Cole's face. When he sat up, she was almost relieved. The position, added to the arm already around her shoulder and the rock-hard thigh aligned with hers, had been much too intimate for comfort.

Not that it had been his intention—Adam was being the quintessential buddy—but Cole's senses were dying a hard death. Just because two people decided to be friends did not mean one stopped feeling and seeing and smelling. At least, not right away.

As she'd done on more than one occasion lately, Cole resorted to humor. She gave her traveling companion a nudge in the ribs with her elbow. "You old-moneyed, well-traveled types are all jaded, did you know that?"

She wasn't prepared for the intimacy of his green-eyed gaze and, being caught off guard, there was nothing Cole could do to prevent the thrill from racing along her spine.

"Maybe you're just what a jaded old-moneyed type like me needs," he said. "Up until now, I guess I'd taken this old city for granted."

"Have you been here that many times?" Cole asked, acutely aware that their eyes had been locked for much too long a time.

Adam seemed to hesitate. "I studied here once . . . a long time ago." Something caught his eye and he turned to look out the window. "We're here."

Cole followed his gaze and gasped when she read the logo on the awning of the grayish-tan building. "You told me we were staying at a pleasant older hotel. This is the Ritz!"

He laughed as he pulled out French francs from his wallet to pay the driver. "The Ritz is a pleasant older hotel."

They stepped out into a dazzling morning sun and were greeted by a formal, very gracious doorman who issued terse instructions to a porter about their bags. Entering the vast lobby of the hotel was like entering another century. Old-world charm and understated elegance flourished amid marble columns, Persian carpets and crystal chandeliers.

Formalities were handled with remarkable speed and civility; soon Cole and Adam were being ushered into their suite. "Oh, my!" Cole uttered for the umpteenth time as she took in every fabulous detail, from the freshly cut flowers to the opulent Louis XV decor of watered-silk pastels.

"Do you like it?" Adam asked, his tone betraying concern. "I know how you feel about Twin Elms. . . ."

Cole whirled around to look at him, feeling like royalty and loving it. "Oh, yes, but this is Paris...the Ritz. They're entitled to be outrageously romantic!" Cole clamped a hand to her mouth. "Oops—you know what I mean."

His eyes crinkled in a smile. "It's all right, Cole. You don't have to be so touchy about what you said. I promise not to throw you out for giving an honest reaction." He tossed his jacket over a chair and went to the heavily draped window. "I thought the Ritz might give you something pleasant to look back on when you're cold and miserable at six thousand feet."

Cole came to his side and looked out at the Place Vendôme with its spired Napoleonic memorial. "That was nice of you, Adam. Thank you."

He turned to her and smiled. "Would you like to rest a while before we launch out to see the sights?"

"Absolutely not! I have my whole life to rest. Right now, I'm going to freshen up and then you're going to show me everything worth seeing in Paris."

"Okay. If you're up to it, so am I."

Cole chose one of the two bedrooms as her own and wasted no time donning a simple turquoise shirtwaist and a comfortable pair of sandals before returning to join Adam.

It was a radiant day, the sky a perfect cloudless azure, when Adam brought Cole through the serene Tuileries garden. The September air was warm, the setting idyllic with shimmering ponds surrounded by chestnut trees and sculptures by Rodin and Maillol. Adam showed her the Place de la Concorde, an enormous square that in two days' time would be the launch site for several dozen gas balloons.

By the time they had passed beneath the Arc de Triomphe and scaled the heights of the Eiffel Tower, Cole was in a state bordering on exhaustion. They were strolling—actually, Cole was limping—along the Champs-Élysées when she admitted that to him. He laughed when she informed him his endurance resembled that of a pack animal.

All of a sudden, Cole's attention was spirited away by a showcase window of the most exquisite hand-painted silk scarves she'd ever seen. "Oh, Adam, look!" she exclaimed, not caring in the least that he probably wouldn't be as captivated as she was by the display.

"Do you like them?" he asked redundantly.

"Ooh" was all she could say.

Adam took her hand and propelled her to the door of the boutique. "Then let's go inside."

Half an hour later, after being cosseted and pampered and served coffee by two genteel French saleswomen, Cole emerged from the shop with three veritable works of art in her bag—mementos of the trip bought for her by Adam. One of the scarves was black silk, delicately painted with white orchids, and it would go perfectly with her dinner dress that evening. Cole could hardly wait to see Adam's reaction, until she remembered her self-imposed rules of decorum. It was all right to dress nicely for dinner; it was not all right for her to pirouette before him like an infatuated teenager.

"Are you ready for a rest now?" Adam asked, apparently unaware of her self-directed remonstrations.

"Oh, yes . . . please."

Adam held out his arm and Cole was more than happy to oblige by taking it. "We're due to meet our ground crew in an hour at a café on the Boulevard Saint-Germain. It's just around the corner, practically."

Cole could only nod, but as she was soon to discover, his "practically" meant another fifteen minutes of brisk hiking. Only Cole's utter fatigue and her gratitude for the scarves prevented her from dropping onto the sidewalk and refusing to go another step. When they were finally seated at the café, enjoying a feast of crusty French bread, pâté and Cinzano, Cole was ready to forgive him the understatement. It was sheer delight to be part of the Parisian milieu, laughing and talking and watching people go by.

Sipping coffee, Cole looked up to find standing at her side a man with the brightest eyes and the blackest skin she had ever seen. The slightly built man gave her a broad smile then turned his attention to Adam. "Congratulations, Doctor. You have been in Paris less than twenty-four hours, and already you have managed to sequester one of the city's most beautiful women."

Adam's healthy laugh rang out as he stood up to greet the man warmly. "Etienne, good to see you again! I hate to disillusion you, but my companion is not French, at least not a purebred. Cole, I'd like you to meet the director of our ground crew, Etienne Lubutu. Etienne, this is *Stargrazer*'s copilot, Cole Jameson."

Etienne took Cole's hand and bowed his head over it with consummate chivalry. "I am very pleased to meet you, Cole. Adam has become most resourceful at selecting his flying partners." His English was exotically accented but impeccable. Cole took an immediate liking to the charming young man.

"How do you do, Etienne? And thank you for the compliment, but I assure you I've been selected solely on the basis of my ability to work hard and keep my mouth shut."

Etienne laughed as he sat down to join them. Cole poured him some coffee while Adam recounted their grueling walking tour of the city to his friend.

Cole was content to listen, entranced by Etienne's melodious English. "Where are you from?" she asked at one point.

"Zaire," he replied.

"Are you here on vacation?"

"Not exactly. I am in Paris to complete my internship, and fortunately was able to acquire free time for this race."

Cole had her chin cupped in one hand. "I'm pretty excited about it myself. I raced once before with the infamous Blackfoot, so I thought I'd risk a repeat performance."

Etienne's expression grew blank. "Black foot?" he repeated. "That is some kind of American good-luck charm, perhaps?"

Adam caught on to his confusion at once and responded with a hearty, appreciative guffaw. "No, Etienne, don't worry. I did not commission you for your black foot." He turned to Cole. "On this side of the Atlantic, I'm known only as Adam. It takes too long to explain the origins of my nickname to people who haven't been raised in the States."

Cole turned crimson and apologized to Etienne, who assured her he took no offense. In fact, when Adam told his friend about growing up with the Algonquin tribe, Etienne laughed uproariously at the gaffe.

Soon they were joined by the other two members of the ground crew. Jean-Pierre was a middle-aged, taciturn sort who worked for the National Weather Bureau and would be their meteorologist for the race. Marc, a much younger man, was to accompany Etienne in the chase car, navigating him through the complex network of French roads.

The time flew as the five of them went over every detail of the race: weather conditions, launch particulars, arrangements for delivery of the helium and a thousand other sundries. Each of the crew members seemed to be unfailingly meticulous. Adam had chosen wisely.

By late afternoon, despite her best efforts, Cole was ready to fall asleep in her plate. Adam took one look at her half-mast eyes and made their excuses to the others, who were quite happy to continue the steady flow of wine and food arriving at their table. It wasn't long before a taxi was speeding Cole and Blackfoot back to their hotel.

"Where would you like to have dinner for your first night in Paris?" Adam asked when they were in the suite.

Through a somnolent haze, Cole smiled and said, "Maxim's, please—if it's okay with you."

"Of course it's okay," he assured her gently. "I want this time to be special for you. We'll take in the Folies-Bergère, too."

She would have loved to throw her arms around him and kiss him for being so sweet, but not only was it unacceptable behavior, she was much too punchy to execute such a complicated maneuver. Cole staggered toward her bedroom. "Wake me up in two hours," she mumbled, and closed the door behind her.

COLE'S EYELIDS SEEMED to be glued shut. She finally had to pry them open with thumb and forefinger and was surprised to see there was still a slice of Parisian sunshine streaming in from behind the drapes.

What, had she only slept a half hour or so? She felt so well-rested. Cole threw back the heavy covers and padded to the window. On her way, she looked down at herself and discovered she was wearing nothing but a bra and panties. How on earth had that happened?

Cole clenched her sleep-dazed head with both hands and tried to think back. The last she remembered was the taxi ride to the hotel. Stepping to one side, Cole drew back the drapes. It was morning!

That would explain the angry rumblings in her stomach. She had missed Maxim's and the Folies-Bergère entirely! And if that wasn't bad enough, she distinctly remembered flopping down on the bed for her nap fully dressed. There was only one person who could have undressed her and put her under the covers last night, a task clearly above and beyond a friend's call of duty.

Cole slid into a striped caftan and went out in search of Adam. He wasn't in the sitting room and his bedroom door was closed. She crossed the room and knocked on his door; there was no answer. She tried again; still no response. Perhaps he had already gone downstairs for breakfast. Cole turned the knob slowly and opened the door.

Adam was sound asleep on the bed, the white linen sheet spiraled around his naked body like a barber pole, leaving his bottom exposed to anyone with the audacity to stare. Cole couldn't help herself. Her fingers were curled around the edge of the door, but she couldn't move. The sight of Adam's sun-bronzed form, exquisitely muscled, disturbingly masculine, made her senses come alive as if from a deep sleep. Her pulse began to hammer from deep within her, and her longing was a physical ache that twisted and turned inside until she thought she'd cry out for need of him.

But of course, all of that was irrelevant. From the ravaged look of the bed, Cole had to assume he'd had a hard time dropping off to sleep. She'd come back for him in an hour—

"Cole, what are you doing in here?" Adam sat bolt upright then became aware of his state of undress. He glanced down to ensure that his lower regions were properly covered, and Cole could have sworn his tawniness deepened a shade or two.

She smiled softly. "Good morning. I didn't mean to startle you. I was just trying to determine what became of my first evening in Paris."

Adam relaxed and returned her smile. Then he lifted both arms to ruffle up his sleep-flattened curls. "You slept through it, while I barely escaped with my life."

"What?"

"When I undressed you and tried to cover you up, you were like a rogue grizzly." He indicated a series of red ridges on one shoulder.

"Oh, no!" Cole cried, bringing her hand to her mouth. "Did I do that? I'm sorry."

"No harm done."

"Did I . . . say anything?" she asked.

The corner of Adam's mouth turned up in a maddeningly evasive look of amusement. "Nothing you need to worry about." He swung his long, muscled legs off the bed, held the sheet around his waist and stood up. "Give me ten minutes and I'll join you for breakfast."

There was little time to linger over the croissants and coffee. The Jean Beauvais race began in less than twenty-four hours and a million things needed to be done. *Stargrazer II* was housed at an elegant old château outside Paris, with extensive grounds on which to lay out the deflated balloon and the vast assortment of equipment. Every item from the compass right down to the plastic coffee mugs had to be weighed and catalogued before being stowed aboard the gondola. The larger items were fastened down, the others stuffed in small places to reduce the clutter. Every inch of the balloon's gas envelope was checked and rechecked for leaks. At last it was determined that *Stargrazer II* was perfect.

Cole assisted Jean-Pierre's wife in the preparation of food for the race, packing it into airtight bags and coolers. That evening, everyone enjoyed a preflight dinner in the grand dining hall of the château. While the others toasted to victory with fine French wine, Cole and Adam clinked crystal goblets of sparkling mineral water.

All through the evening, Cole was aware that she and Adam were somehow detached from the good-natured ribaldry around them. It was a strange feeling, but one she liked. Perhaps it was because tomorrow there would only be the two of them at *Stargrazer*'s helm, facing the perils and the thrills of wind-powered flight. A delicious shiver of anticipation ran through Cole's body. If the fates were kind, she and Adam would have forty-eight hours together with no mundane intrusions, no earthbound realities . . . only each other.

Beyond that, nothing mattered.

DISTANT THUNDER rumbled angrily on the morning of the Jean Beauvais race. Overnight, Paris had turned bone-chilling cold; the clouds blanketing the city were so low they looked as though the cathedral spires might pierce them. The balloonists, their ground crews and thousands of spectators milled restlessly, waiting for the inevitable deluge.

Adam was stalking the pavement near *Stargrazer*, his ruddy face creased with impatience. "That cloud ceiling can't be any more than fifteen hundred feet. It'd be lunatic to launch in this weather."

"I agree," Etienne said, shivering and rubbing his arms briskly. "Let me go and speak with the officials. Perhaps they are considering postponement of the launch."

Cole, blowing on her fingers, hopped from one foot to another and watched Etienne disappear into the crowd of dismal aeronauts. Fortunately, she had packed a quilted parka in her luggage, though it had been intended for high-altitude flight, not for prelaunch on the Place de la Concorde.

"I think it's a lousy idea to postpone the launch," Cole offered, though her opinion had not been sought.

Adam, his eyes slits, was scanning the skyline for a break in the cloud cover. "You're right," he said. "The race ought to be cancelled altogether."

"Oh, for heaven's sake," Cole sputtered through half-frozen lips. "Jean-Pierre said this was a localized weather system; we could be out of it in an hour. Waiting around only makes things worse. We're losing so much helium with the balloons buffeting against each other that none of us will be able to last forty-eight hours aloft."

Ridges of annoyance lined Adam's brow. "I am quite aware of that, Cole, but in this weather most of us won't get any further than the end of the plaza, which doesn't do a hell of a lot for the spirit of competition, either. I, for one, have greater aspirations for *Stargrazer II* than the successful crossing of the Place de la Concorde."

Cole lanced him with a look of irritation that went totally unnoticed. He really was being unreasonably stubborn this morning, she thought peevishly. "Listen, I've seen weather like this in Pennsylvania," she said. "No sooner would they postpone the launch and deflate the balloons than the clouds would break and the sun would come out. And even if the storm does come, we could be past it in no time." Inwardly, Cole knew that belaboring her point was futile as the final decision rested with the judges, not with them. But preflight adrenaline seemed to be making both of them unusually irascible this morning.

Etienne returned a few minutes later. "The launching is to begin at once!" he announced. "*Stargrazer II* is directly after *Paris* and immediately before *Rio de Janeiro*."

Cole suppressed an exclamation of triumph at the judges' decision, limiting her response to a quiet sigh of relief. As she and Adam conducted the preflight check, they deftly avoided meeting each other's eyes.

When all was made ready and they were on board the gondola, the two of them watched the other balloons attempt to launch. Plagued with downdrafts, updrafts and cyclonic winds, virtually no one managed a flawless ascent. Mexico City's entry, festooned with eagles and serpents, slammed against the pavement mere seconds after making what had appeared to be the first perfect launch.

"See, Adam? Look what happened to them!" Cole said, resurrecting an argument they'd abandoned an hour earlier. "I think we should ballast right away and get above the clouds as soon as we can."

His scathing expression confirmed he was still not sold on the idea. "Thank you for your input, but I'm still the pilot and I have no intention of wasting precious sand this early in the race."

Cole clamped her mouth shut angrily and rivetted her attention to the launch of the Parisian balloon, an ornate sphere of sapphire blue and gilt fleurs-de-lis. She watched with immense satisfaction as the crew ballasted furiously and rose on a perfect and steady column of air. That's it, she thought! That's what they ought to do! But just when it seemed the French balloon was nearing equilibrium, the crew stopped ballasting and the balloon lurched groundward with terrifying force. In order to avoid touching ground and being disqualified, they had to dump more sand, squandering far more than they could afford. The Parisians would never make it to the end of the race now.

If Cole was hoping Adam might learn from the mistakes of others, she was mistaken. He gave the terse order to launch while Cole held her breath and offered up a silent prayer. She waited hopefully for an order to ballast, but of course none came. There was no team effort between them this morning, and each of them was seething silently at his post as if he were on board alone. There was no magic in the launch, no aura of serenity. All was overshadowed by the impending storm, taut nerves and the undeniable element of danger.

Fortunately, *Stargrazer* was anxious to ride the wind that would have shredded her to ticker tape if she'd stayed tethered much longer, so she took matters into her own hands. In fits and starts, she lumbered skyward, straining to reach the low, gray ceiling of clouds. But without the sun's heat to expand the helium and make her rise, *Stargrazer* couldn't do her name justice. They reached equilibrium much too soon.

They cleared the buildings surrounding the plaza with a reasonable margin of safety, but Cole's blood did not stop racing. As long as they were flying over Paris and under cirrus clouds, they would not be safe.

Adam's mouth was set in a thin line as his eyes moved ceaselessly across their impending flight path. Cole had the distinct impression he was avoiding her—no small feat in a space the size of the gondola. But knowing there was little she could do for the time being, she concentrated on the instrument panel that measured their altitude and their rate of ascent. So far, they weren't climbing worth a hoot.

"Cole, get down *quick!*"

Instinctively, Cole obeyed the order and hunkered down beside Adam, her heart pounding with unnamed fear. In the seconds that followed, there was an angry, labored creaking of ropes and they plowed head-on into the side of a glass-and-steel skyscraper. *Stargrazer*'s gargantuan gas envelope collided like a ponderous beluga whale against the facade of steel and concrete, and she was pinned captive by the force of the winds.

Her gondola and its passengers, as per the laws of inertia, continued their flight path, swinging into the side of the building with a velocity that would surely destroy the gondola and send Cole and Adam plummeting to their deaths. Horrified, Cole peered over the side to find her face within inches of a huge plate-glass window. She squeezed her eyes shut, waiting for the shatter. But less than an inch away from impact, the gondola reached the limits of her rigging and swung back like a giant pendulum. Despite the reprieve, neither Cole nor Adam dared move, but braced themselves for the next inevitable swing toward the building.

It didn't happen. With a shift of wind, *Stargrazer* loosed herself from her obstacle and rolled around the surface of the building until she was free to resume her course. And, as if she knew how to avoid another mishap, *Stargrazer* climbed higher and flew on, apparently none the worse for wear.

A hundred lifetimes seemed to pass before Cole felt safe enough to get to her feet. It was the closest brush she'd ever had with her own mortality and as she huddled like a frightened animal in the corner of the gondola, her frenzied imagination continued to plague her.

"It's all right now, Cole," Adam tried to assure her, kneeling at her side and rubbing her back briskly to quell the tremors. "We're safe, I promise you."

She looked up at him doubtfully. "But what if *Stargrazer*'s developed a leak . . . or the air ducts are damaged?"

"Stop worrying," he said softly, pulling her close to him and bringing her to her feet without her realizing it. "No damage was done. We'd have known about it by now."

Cole clung to Adam and let the tears of release spill over her cheeks. Gradually her breathing steadied. As long as she didn't let her thoughts drift back to their brush with death, she'd be all right. And as long as Adam continued to hold her and stroke her hair, she knew nothing could hurt her again.

"We're past Paris now," he told her in gentle, soothing tones. "There's blue sky up ahead." Then he pulled away and his hands closed over her shoulders. "Cole, if I'd listened to you, if we'd ballasted right away, this never would have happened. I don't know how to apologize, but I do know I was wrong."

Remorse clouded Adam's eyes and his face was etched with anguish—emotions so profound they overrode the straggling remnants of Cole's own fear. She felt no satisfaction, only immense gratitude to a higher power that they had been spared the ultimate consequences of his rare lapse of good judgment.

Cole lifted her hands to her shoulders and slipped her fingers beneath Adam's palms. For the first time since she'd known him, his hands were cold and damp; a shudder rippled through her. Her heart swelled and the brittle shell of self-restraint she'd lived with these past weeks shattered.

"Let's not even think about it," she said. "We're alive . . . and we're together. Nothing else matters."

The progression seemed as natural and as complementary as the colors of a spectrum, the expressions in Adam's eyes flowing from fear to contrition to gratitude and at last to searing intimacy. When their bodies came together, when their mouths sought solace from each other, this too seemed part of a totally natural progression of events.

Adam murmured Cole's name against her mouth, angling his lips and thrusting to satiate his need. Cole felt herself relax fully, glorying in the half-forgotten sensations of being in his arms, the masculine scent and taste that was uniquely his, the fullness of his mouth, the cool crispness of his curls under her fingers.

Oh, how she loved him! Now that she was once again experiencing the full flowering of his rapture, Cole knew her feelings had not abated. In her valiant attempts to deny them, she had learned to live with the constant dull ache of his absence, to work around it as best she could. But then, being in Paris, the ache had intensified to a painful, bittersweet longing, one that his slightest touch threatened to ignite at any time.

Now they were in a sun-drenched heaven belonging only to them, and even Adam seemed aware of the magic. "I've missed you so much," he growled softly against her ear. "When we were apart, I could never quite grasp the memory of how good you felt in my arms. Perhaps I didn't want to...." A soft choking sound came from his throat—a lonely sound.

Cole tilted her head back to place her finger on his lips. "Shh, this time is all ours. Let's not waste it with regrets." Her words were as much a consolation to herself as to Adam. Here in this special realm of an airborne balloon they were free to let down their protective guards, break loose from the chains of reason, secure in the knowledge that the here and now was all-pervasive.

Cole shrugged herself out of the quilted parka; she no longer needed it in the clear, midmorning sunshine. Sliding her hands up to Adam's shoulders, she eased off his heavy wool jacket, and as she silently unfastened the buttons of his shirt, she rose to her toes and kissed him. Confidence soared through her like a wild bird in flight. She didn't need to hear any words to know there was love in Adam's eyes.

Her pilot, entranced, was more than willing to afford her the role of commander in their long-denied rediscovery of each other. He leaned back against the side of the gondola, his mouth turned up slightly in a smile as Cole moved her palms against the shirtless expanse of his chest.

She drew in a sharp breath as her fingertips explored the solid framework of muscle and sinew, and her relentless stimulation of Adam's senses urged an elemental response. He moaned softly, cradled Cole's head in his hands and kissed her hair. She looked up and smiled while her fingers crept down to unfasten the snap of his jeans and lower the zipper.

A searing tingle rushed along her arms when her hands rode the length of his rock-hard thighs, coaxing the snug pant legs down. Then she knelt to untie his soft kidskin shoes and remove his socks.

Adam stood before her dressed only in cotton briefs, his physical state obvious through the thin fabric. "Let me do the same for you," he entreated in a voice thick with passion.

"Not yet," whispered Cole, her own waves of response as unbridled as his, yet brought about solely by giving him pleasure. She moved her body to his and kissed him fully, exploring the crests and hollows of his mouth, nuzzling herself to him in a highly provocative interplay of flesh and fabric.

After she had savored Adam's mouth, Cole moved to the planes and angles of his face, her lips and tongue tracing the crags and the worry lines that were bristly with the hint of whiskers never totally tamed. He was so rugged, so intrinsically male that he took Cole's breath away.

Her mouth continued its journey along his neck, bronzed and ropy, giving way at last to the springy brown mat of his chest. Cole was thrilled to feel the shudder of his body as she flicked and nipped and teased him to new heights of passion.

Stargrazer glided like an old clipper ship, her rigging creaking and rubbing as she continued to carry them sunward. Please keep us on a safe course for a while yet, Cole exhorted silently to the balloon. We need this time so much, he and I. As if she understood, *Stargrazer* slowed then leveled off to a steady course.

Cole went on to map the taut contours of Adam's torso with her hands. Tasting the web of downy hair that narrowed to a single line on his stomach, she dipped her tongue briefly into his navel and smiled at the respondent lick of flame in her own body.

Her fingers slipped beneath his briefs and lowered them along flawless legs. She knelt down once more to gaze on their virile perfection. She wrapped her arms around them and rained a string of tiny electric kisses down Adam's thigh, past his knee, along his calf until she came to his feet. Her tongue grazed his instep, tickled his arch and traced the long lines of each toe before crossing to the other foot and journeying upwards. In her fiercely determined seduction, Cole left no part of his body untouched.

Then, understanding well the sweet physical agony she had wrought on her lover's body, Cole divested herself swiftly of her own slacks and blouse, slipping out of her undergarments before pulling him down to the deck of the gondola. Assuming one final vestige of control, she urged Adam onto his back. Every fiber of Cole's body was ablaze as he filled her with himself, her every thought crying out in exultation at the sweet renewal of their union.

She dug her nails into his shoulders; her hair fell across crimson cheeks burning with unabashed desire. Adam's hands held her hips lightly, guiding her but still affording her the rare and special conquest of his body. Such a wonderful, willing lover, she thought, her heart bursting.

Their crescendo rose in tandem, its fiery refrain building and building until it could build no higher. For a dazzling eternity, they lingered, hovering on an ecstatic peak as the wind lifted them past marshmallow castles and oceans of azure sky. Then, at last, like two arrows in flight, they drifted down—spent and joyous—to clasp each other in welcoming arms.

For a long while, adrift on a current of air, they lay together not knowing where they were headed and caring even less. Or perhaps it was not such a long while, for time was a meaningless entity there on the deck of *Stargrazer II*. At six thousand feet traveling at an undetermined speed, the past and the future held slight significance.

Later, after they were dressed, Cole was confirming their flight direction with the compass when she turned to Adam. "May I ask you a personal question?"

"Go ahead," he said as he scanned the distant cloud formations.

She felt the splash of color on her cheekbones. It was really such a silly question, after all. "Have you ever made love in a balloon before?"

"No," Adam replied, laughing gently. "Was it your first time, too?"

Cole nodded and felt much better. She put the compass down and went to look over the side of the gondola. Far below them, the cloud layer still blanketed much of the countryside, but there were breaks now and again that gave them a glimpse of the rich greens and golds of harvest.

"We're heading due south, by the way," Cole said.

"I figured as much. Obviously, we're still caught up in the pressure system that brought about the storm. So much for my plans for landing in Germany. How do you feel about breakfast in Spain the day after tomorrow?"

"That sounds wonderful," Cole answered, her imagination dallying with an image of them landing somewhere deep in the Pyrenees, in an impenetrable forest with a babbling brook nearby, an abandoned cottage... Oh well, she thought with a laugh, there was no harm in daydreaming.

Stargrazer kept a straight course for the remainder of the day; in fact, she practically flew herself. By nightfall, Cole was woozy with exhaustion, and the autumn air held a chill that several layers of wool clothing could not dispel.

"I'll take the first watch," Adam announced as they finished drinking their tea. "It's time you got some sleep."

Cole saw fatigue shadowing his eyes. "Why don't you go first?"

He shook his head firmly. "I'm not very tired yet. Don't worry, I'm not so noble that I'll let you sleep past your watch."

With that final reassurance, Cole was more than happy to follow orders, crawling fully dressed beneath the covered portion of the deck into a cozy sleeping bag.

She could have sworn no more than a few minutes had passed when she felt Adam nudging her awake. "Cole, it's four a.m. Are you ready to handle a watch?"

Her spirit was willing, but Cole's body steadfastly refused to leave the snug confines of the thermal sleeping bag; her eyelids felt like lead curtains. Sleeping on board a silent, floating balloon was like being encased in a tree-hanging cocoon, and she felt not unlike a reluctant caterpillar.

"Okay, I'm awake," she mumbled at last, sheer force of will inducing her sleepy limbs to action. "But hurry up and crawl into the bag while it's still warm." Cole wriggled out and moved aside to make room for Adam. She was about to get up when he reached out and brought her into his arms.

"Don't go yet," he said. "Let me hold you for a few minutes."

Smiling, Cole nestled down beside him, resting her head on his shoulder. She was content to do nothing but listen to his deep and regular breathing.

"How could I have been so stupid as to refuse to let you fly with me?" Adam murmured between yawns.

Cole brushed his cheek with a soft kiss. "Damned if I know," she teased.

Her lover's response was a throaty snore; he was fast asleep.

THE SUN'S RAYS cast a diaphanous morning veil over the hills and the vineyards and the picturesque villages of Bordeaux. Cole leaned out of the gondola as far as she could and breathed deeply of the clean, crisp air. What an incredible way to savor the beauty of France, drifting above it with the sounds of songbirds for accompaniment.

Adam was still asleep, and Cole was loath to disturb his much-needed rest. Now that daylight was finally here, she felt refreshed and exhilarated; but there had been a time before dawn, when the night was at its blackest, when she'd felt a little frightened and more alone than she'd ever felt in her life.

"What's going on out here?" Adam muttered in a sleep-thickened voice, crawling out onto the open deck. "I should have been awake hours ago."

Cole poured a cup of coffee for him from the thermos she'd prepared earlier. "I know, but you looked so peaceful I didn't have the heart to wake you."

"You're a kindhearted fool," he rebuked softly, taking her in his arms for a kiss.

Cole thought he looked positively endearing this morning, rumpled and wrinkled and slightly disoriented. His cheeks were shaded with grayish-auburn stubble that gave him a slightly disreputable air, in marked contrast to his clear green eyes. "Did you have any problems during the night?" he asked after taking a sip of coffee.

"None at all. We descended to one thousand feet just before dawn, but I thought I'd try waiting until the sun came up before ballasting. As it turned out, the heat was enough to bring us back up to two thousand feet, and we appear to have stabilized."

"Good show," Adam said, his gaze filled with admiration. "You did exactly the right thing."

Cole tried to brush off the praise, but frankly, she was delighted. "Care for some breakfast?"

"Mmm, by all means. How about crepes suzette, sausages . . . maybe some hash browns?"

"Ha! Dream on!" Cole tossed back. "You'll make do with continental. Fortunately, Jean-Pierre's wife makes wonderful croissants and blackberry preserves. You won't starve."

Cole prepared his breakfast while Adam rolled up the sleeping bag." I hope you don't mind if I forgo the razor for the next day or so," he told her when he sat down to eat. "I live in dread of hitting a wind shear just when the blade is poised at my jugular."

She ran her hand over his cheek, enjoying the feel of rugged bristles. "I can live with it, but careful where you aim it."

Cole took coffee for herself and watched the passing scenery. A meandering river was charting an unhurried course, running as placidly as *Stargrazer's* flight. The undulating land was dappled in a palette of earth tones with patches of wildflowers brilliant against their verdant backdrop. The Bordeaux countryside seemed to harbor the same genteel qualities as its residents were purported to possess; it was charming, rustic and unassuming as a loaf of French bread.

Off in the distance, Cole spotted a young couple riding bicycles along a narrow wooded lane. They blended so well with their surroundings they reminded Cole of a painting by Seurat.

"Adam, look over there," Cole said, pointing to the couple. "Don't they look like they're having a good time?"

Bringing his coffee cup, he came to join her. "They sure do. If I weren't up here doing what I'm doing, I'd settle for being down there doing what they're doing." His arm slipped around Cole's waist and he drew her closer.

Suddenly, their tranquillity was spliced by an earpiercing scream and it took both of them a moment or two to realize where the sound had come from. Adam look over the side. The young woman had fallen from her bicycle and was lying huddled on the stone road.

"Good Lord, I think she's pregnant!" he exclaimed.

Cole peered toward the site of the fall and couldn't imagine how Adam had been able to discern such a detail at this distance. When she turned to ask him about it, she was staggered by the sudden transformation of her pilot. His face had taken on an intensity she'd never seen before, as if some stronger force compelled him to toss aside his coffee cup and delve into the storage section for his medical bag. In an instant, Blackfoot had become Dr. Adam Torrie.

By now the woman's husband had alighted from his bicycle and was at her side, looking around helplessly as he tried to console her. But there was no traffic on the lonely road, not so much as a farmhouse nearby. There was no one except the airborne crew of *Stargrazer II*.

"We're landing!" Adam announced brusquely.

"But—"

The look he gave her left no room for discussion. It would do Cole no good to waste precious seconds pointing out that landing was a good idea, since the woman obviously needed help, but there were no safe clearings below them to land in.

"Hold the vent line open," Adam ordered, taking up a megaphone that hung inside the gondola. "Hello!" he shouted. "Hello!"

The young man looked around in confusion then traced the source of the voice to the skies above him. He waved his arms and shouted back. *"Ma femme! Elle est enceinte!"* Even at this distance, his distress was audible.

Stargrazer was already descending rapidly and Cole wondered what—besides holding the vent line open—she was supposed to be doing. Everywhere she looked, there were trees. The only clearing was the narrow stone road, which was really of no use at all. If they'd been flying in the same direction as the road, it could conceivably have been used as a landing strip. But it was almost exactly perpendicular to their flight path, and unless Adam pitched in to help soon, they were going to fly right past everything.

"Je viens!" Adam hollered out in fluent French. *"Je suis médecin!"*

That was all the young man needed to hear. He gestured happily, then returned his attention to his wife while Adam resumed command of the balloon. "You're doing fine, Cole."

"But the trees!" she protested, not at all happy with their collision course. "How do we get the balloon to turn when we reach the road?"

"We don't. When we get near the spot where the forest breaks for the road, we'll hit the trees to slow our descent. Then, just as we pass over the road, I'll pull the rip line. Hold on tight, flex your knees and protect your head."

Not a second remained to explain further. They were plummeting swiftly toward the ancient shade trees, though the dirt road still looked no wider than a ruler. Before Cole could blink, they had reached the edge of the tree line. The gondola hit the trees, bouncing hard off a gnarled limb and jerking back up slightly. So far, so good.

"Hold on!" Adam pulled the rip line and the gas envelope collapsed into itself.

As he predicted, the trees had cushioned their descent, but there was still a fifty-foot drop without benefit of helium. Cole rolled herself into a ball in one corner of the gondola and held her breath, waiting for the crash. One second passed . . . two . . . With a horrendous crunching noise and a gut-churning lurch, *Stargrazer*'s envelope caught in the trees, leaving the gondola and its occupants swaying some six feet above the hard ground. When the swaying stopped, the balloon still had not let go.

After a time, Adam motioned to Cole. "You get out first, and when you land get clear of the gondola right away. No telling how long it'll hold."

Obediently, Cole uncurled her body and stood up on shaky legs. Being careful not to jostle the precarious gondola any more than necessary, she swung one leg over the side, then the other, and jumped to the ground. She moved quickly from the gondola and turned around to look up. An enormous poplar along with two neighboring trees held the splayed helium bag in place as effectively as if it were on a giant pitchfork.

"It's okay!" Cole called out. "*Stargrazer* can't go anywhere."

Moments later, Adam had joined her on the the ground, but they wasted no time on each other, both knowing instinctively they were okay. Cole followed behind him as he rushed up the road to the woman's side, his medical bag in hand.

The woman looked very young, no more than eighteen. Petite and dark-haired, she would have been pretty under other circumstances, but now her face was ashen, and despite the cool morning air perspiration beaded her forehead.

Adam conversed with her and her husband. "She's not due for another six weeks," he explained to Cole, "but she's definitely in labor."

"What do we do?" she asked, feeling hopelessly unqualified to handle this situation.

Adam glanced around. "First, we'll get her off the road. We'll bring her down to that clearing by the river."

The husband assisted in carrying his wife to the glade. Cole busied herself by steering the bicycles out of harm's way.

"Can you start a fire?" Adam asked when she came to join them.

Cole blanched. "With two sticks?"

"There are matches in my bag," he informed her, grinning.

"Okay." Cole set off to gather bits of wood for kindling. It had been a long time since Girl Scouts, but with any luck, the pressure would jog her memory.

The young woman was already beginning to relax as Adam demonstrated how she should breathe and gently encouraged her. Cole was the one who could hardly bear it each time the woman had a contraction.

"She's nearly fully dilated," Adam stated, as if Cole was the attending obstetrical nurse and actually had some idea what he was talking about. "But she still has a lot of work ahead of her."

Cole poked at the fire with dogged concentration. "Will she be able to do it?"

"I don't know," he admitted. "At least if we were in the hospital, we'd have the option of doing a cesarean."

The little fire was now burning steadily. "Do you want me to boil water?" she asked, desperately trying to remember what she'd seen in movies.

"Yes, and we'll need clean linens." Adam stopped short when he realized what he was asking of her.

"It's all right," Cole replied quickly. "I can get back into the gondola." Without waiting for an answer, she hurried up the hill to the disabled balloon. Uttering a silent prayer of thanks for her newly acquired strength, Cole jumped up and grasped a ring near the base of the gondola. Her weight caused it to sway wildly. She hung on, waiting for the motion to subside, then pulled herself up with the series of rings specifically designed for emergency use. Her arms protested the exertion, but they held up. Soon she was able to swing one leg into the suspended gondola.

After locating towels, clean clothes, cooking pots and anything else she imagined might be of use, Cole stuffed it all into a hemp bag. She was about to start climbing down when she noticed the bottle of champagne tucked into the instrument panel. The champagne was meant to be shared with the owners of the landing site, but Cole decided they could break with tradition under the circumstances. Smiling, she tucked the bottle into the bag and left the gondola.

By the time Cole got back to the glade, the woman's contractions were less than a minute apart and it was all her husband and Adam could do to keep her calm. She squeezed the men's fingers until they were white, clenched her teeth and then swore in French when the pains subsided.

Cole put water on to boil, then went over to join them. Trying to suppress her own sympathetic nausea, she asked, "Is there anything else I can do?"

Adam wiped the woman's brow and shook his head. "Not yet. I gave her a small swig of brandy from my medical bag, and she proclaimed it the worst rotgut she'd ever had."

"What kind was it?" asked Cole.

"Don't know. Generic, I think."

Cole chuckled. "What did you expect? We're probably no more than fifty miles from Cognac."

The young woman seemed to be holding out better than her husband. He could no longer bear the sight of his wife in so much pain and was pacing the riverbank, chain-smoking.

"He says they don't have prenatal classes in their village," explained Adam, "and he probably wouldn't have gone if they did."

Cole made an appropriate remark about the man's Neanderthal attitude. Then, trying to make the woman feel better, she regaled her with fractured French and smiled a lot.

"Okay, she's ready." Adam called the husband back and instructed him on how to support his wife during the birth. "Cole, I'd like you to hold the woman's shoulders or her hands—whatever she prefers. She's tiring quickly and she needs something solid to work against for these few final pushes."

The woman panted shallowly while everyone else assumed their positions for the next contraction. Cole's heart rose to her throat and she was amazed at how the woman was able to draw on some inner reserve to give a hearty push.

"Brava!" Cole exclaimed, not knowing what other word would be understood. The woman glanced up at Cole and there was a brief flicker of amusement in her weary eyes.

"The head is out! *Très bien, madame!*" Adam's excitement mounted. "*Encore une fois!* One more time... *Bien! Voici, vous avez un fils!* Cole, look, it's a boy!"

CHAMPAGNE WAS FLOWING when Etienne and Marc finally arrived, frantic with worry. They'd seen *Stargrazer* drop out of sight and had tried to radio, getting no response. For hours, they'd combed the back roads of Bordeaux, searching for some sign of the disabled balloon and her crew.

Blackfoot apologized to his ground crew, then introduced them to Monsieur and Madame Leclerc, who proudly showed off their new son. The raisin-faced little dream with the frizz of black hair slept in his mother's arms, swaddled in a red-gingham tablecloth.

Moments later, mother and son were lying comfortably in the back of the chase car, a station wagon. Adam and Monsieur Leclerc kept a close eye on things from the back seat, while the others sat in the front. The Leclerc's bicycles rode on the roof.

"What will become of *Stargrazer*?" Marc asked.

"I told the Leclercs they could salvage her and turn her into a family monument," Adam replied, smiling.

IN THE WAITING ROOM of the hospital, Cole and Etienne were sipping coffee while Adam conferred with the obstetrician in the ward. Now and again, Etienne would shake his head. Finally, he declared, "I think I've experienced enough ballooning adventures to last me a lifetime. I shall be glad to retire to a quiet life of medicine."

Cole stretched her arms over her head to relieve the kinks and laughed. "Right at this moment, I appreciate your sentiments. But it was kind of exciting watching Adam at work. He must be a wonderful doctor."

"Ah, that he is. I look forward to working with him again."

Just then, the lounge doors swung open and Adam strode in, beaming. "You will be pleased to hear that young Adam Leclerc weighs in at a strapping five pounds and doesn't even need a respirator. His mother's convinced it's because he was born outdoors."

"Congratulations!" Cole and Etienne exclaimed in unison.

"And a namesake, besides," Cole added. "You should be proud."

Adam gave her a broad grin. "You should be, too. His middle name is Nicolas." He put an arm around each of his friends' shoulders. "Come on. Let's go celebrate."

The bistro they decided on was quiet and unpretentious, with linen-covered tables and copper ornaments on plaster walls. After a few toasts, Etienne excused himself to join Marc at the *pension*. Cole and Adam were alone.

"Etienne thinks you're a pretty admirable doctor," Cole remarked after a moment or two of silence. She was feeling sad all of a sudden, deflated, as though all of the good times and the high times of her life were over. Nothing loomed ahead except a blank, lonely future. She could hardly bear to think about it.

Adam twirled his wineglass absently. "Etienne's one of our finest doctors and he's a good friend. He's gotten me through a lot of rough times." He looked up. "By the way, he thinks the world of you. Says you fit in easily with people."

Unaccountably, Cole blushed. "That was a nice thing for him to say." It was definitely time to change the subject. If they didn't stop talking about friendships, she was going to burst into tears. Cole thought back determinedly to the happy arrival of Adam Nicolas Leclerc. Just remembering the event gave her a warm glow inside. "Adam, wasn't Madame Leclerc wonderfully brave about having her baby under those conditions?"

The sudden change in Adam's expression was almost frightening. "It's no big deal, I assure you," he said. "Millions of women have their babies outside, with no cushy follow-up at a hospital."

Cole's jaw dropped. "What a cruel, insensitive thing to say!"

He shrugged. "I'm only stating a fact."

"And all of that encouragement and support you were giving her while she was in labor was just well-rehearsed jargon, I suppose?"

"It's part of my job, yes," he admitted evenly.

Cole didn't bother the waiter to refill her glass; she snatched the bottle from the table and poured herself a generous bracer. "I can't believe what I'm hearing. I never thought you of all people would have such an archaic, chauvinistic attitude toward childbirth."

Adam returned her challenging glare without apology. "No, that's where you're wrong. What's archaic and chauvinistic is people in the third world continuing to have more babies than they can feed while the developed nations, with their two point three overfed children per family, use foreign aid as a political weapon and dump their surplus grain into the ocean. I'm not against babies, Cole. In fact, I'm entirely on their side."

"So what's your answer?" Cole tossed back indignantly. "Mass sterilization for all of your female patients? I may not be an expert on the subject, but I do know that raising children is supposed to be the most precious experience of a woman's life. And in most parts of the world children are a woman's greatest hope and joy. Who the hell are you to sit on your pedestal and make value judgments about who's entitled to kids and who's not?"

Adam leaned closer, his eyes snapping. "First of all, Cole, I don't sit on a pedestal. I usually stand when I'm working, right in the middle of where it's all happening. What you refer to as a woman's hope and joy is, to many of my patients, just another unwanted mouth to feed. Children cause a drop in the family income while the woman is recovering from childbirth. They bring down her life expectancy because she has a baby every year and doesn't have the nutritional stores to withstand the physical strain. Added to all of that *joy* is the likelihood that one out of every five of her kids will be dead before his first birthday, and that's a conservative estimate. One out of five, Cole. Imagine a village with a thousand people, and think about how many children they have to bury each year."

Cole lowered her eyes. "I'm sorry" was all she could say. Adam knew what he was talking about. If anyone was sitting on a high and mighty pedestal, it was her.

He swallowed the last of his wine and motioned for the check. "I wasn't being critical. Go ahead and have your babies, with my blessing. You'll make a great mother." Then he paused and his tone softened. "Maybe you could even make me a godfather some day... for old times' sake."

Cole lifted her eyes and she saw a tear slip down Adam's craggy cheek.

"COULD YOU TRY the last line again?" Cole requested of the sultry blond singer on the other side of the glass. "The word *splurge* came out a little muddy."

With a slight pout and a toss of her mane, the girl repeated the jingle in her Marilyn Monroe coo. "Chocolite candy ba-a-r...the big splurge with the small price!"

"Very good, Sonia, thank you!" Cole said into the microphone. She turned to the fellow beside her at the mixing board. "What do you think, Ken?"

"Not bad, not bad at all." There was a knock at the door and Ken whirled around. "Now who the hell ... Don't people know this is a recording studio?" He stomped to the door and flung it open. "Can't you read signs—"

The studio receptionist stood her ground unapologetically. "I know, Ken, it's a closed session, but I have an urgent message for Cole."

Cole got up from her chair. "What is it, Rita?"

"Mr. Fawcett called and wants you in his office right away."

"Did you tell him I was in the middle of a commercial?"

"I did, but he said nothing could possibly be more important than what he had to tell you."

Cole groaned. Nothing was ever more important than Alastair Fawcett's most immediate thought. She stooped to pick up her briefcase and purse. "Thanks, Rita. If he calls in the next six and one half minutes, tell him I'm on my way." She turned. "Sorry about this, Ken, but I never know when it's going to be my pink slip."

"No problem," he replied. "I'll call you when I have it all together."

When Cole stepped into Alastair Fawcett's enormous office, she unconsciously wrinkled her nose. Something in the room reminded her of a funeral parlor. She wondered if her gaunt, pasty-faced employer somehow contributed to the effect.

"You wanted to see me, Mr. Fawcett?" she inquired politely.

"Yes, sit down, Miss Jameson." With a bony hand, he gestured toward a chair, baring yellow teeth in what was meant to be a smile. "Now why don't you tell me what it is you see here on my desk." He was never one to squander time and money on preliminaries.

Cole's eyes moved to the antique rosewood desk and she had to swallow a yelp of laughter. "It would appear to be four rolls of toilet paper, sir."

"You are absolutely right. However, these are not just any lavatory tissue," he informed her, pronouncing the word *tissue* with an aristocratic flare of his nostrils. "Smell this one, for example." He handed her a roll gaudily embossed with vines and purple flowers.

Cole obediently sniffed. "Lavender."

"Precisely. Now this one."

Cole took the roll with the palm trees and curling waves. "Uh . . . coconut."

"Correct. Now this."

"Lemon," she answered, deciding the pattern of pale-yellow blossoms was by far the least offensive.

"And finally number four." He handed her the last roll.

Cole smelled it and nearly gagged. The design of bamboo lattice did little to reveal the associated scent. "I'm afraid this one has me stumped, sir."

"Heh-heh-heh." Fawcett gave his version of a laugh. "It had me baffled for a bit, as well. I told the boys they'd have to work on it some more." He retrieved the roll from her and placed it beside the others. "It's musk."

"I see." Cole shuddered and wondered why they hadn't imprinted herds of wandering musk-ox on it instead of bamboo.

"Now, Miss Jameson, how did you feel about the texture of these tissues?"

Cole stared down at her lap and recrossed her legs. For this, she had been summoned from the studio! "I . . . I, uh, don't recall anything unusual about the texture."

Alastair Fawcett looked hurt. "Didn't you? Then here, feel it again."

She leaned over and rubbed a piece of the tissue between her thumb and forefinger, battling an urge to scream. "It feels . . . very nice," she said, having not the foggiest notion of what he was driving at.

Mr. Fawcett knotted his sparse brows, apparently bewildered by Cole's obdurate attitude. He leaned forward and mouthed his words with exaggerated succinctness. "What fabric is most lavatory tissue constantly attempting to emulate, Miss Jameson?"

"Uh, cotton, I guess."

"That's it! Cotton!" He resumed a modicum of control in his voice. "Now we all know that lavatories— that is to say, bathrooms—are assuming an increasingly important role in people's lives today, what with jacuzzis, Roman tubs, bidets, that sort of thing."

He refused to continue until Cole had responded with, "Yes, that's true."

"So, does it not stand to reason these upwardly mobile young professionals would prefer to have their entire decor reflect their newfound affluence? What I mean is, why be content with cotton when one can have silk!"

Cole blinked several times. "Silk?"

He looked at Cole as if she were dim-witted. "Of course, isn't it brilliant? Scented silk lavatory tissue for today's modern bathrooms. Easily the most innovative breakthrough of the decade."

"Yes, I'm sure."

Alastair Fawcett heaved a triumphant sigh. "I knew you'd appreciate the spirit of the venture. The moment I stepped out of the meeting with our prospective—and very important—clients, I thought, what better person to take on this campaign than our very own Miss Jameson?"

Why didn't the floor just open up and swallow her? "You'd like me to handle it, sir?"

"Now don't be modest, my dear. All of us here at Fawcett and Lloyd know and appreciate your keen abilities."

Cole nodded, her mind racing. "Oh . . . yes, thank you, Mr. Fawcett, for your kind vote of confidence. In fact . . . I'm beginning to feel inspired just sitting here. Would you mind if I dashed back to my office for my, er . . . notebook, so I won't forget a single thing that's gone on in our meeting here this morning?"

"Not at all!" Mr. Fawcett leaned back benevolently in his chair. "You go get your notebook and whatever else you need. I have set aside the next half hour just for you."

"Thank you." Cole stood up and backed toward the door, inclining her head as she left, feeling as though she was leaving the presence of demented royalty. When the door was closed behind her, she took a deep breath, nodded at his secretary and strode to her office at the far end of the hall.

She tried not to think too much, concentrating solely on moving quickly. First, she removed the two framed diplomas from the wall and placed them in her brief-case. Then she packed the photograph of her and Adam in front of *Stargrazer II*. From the middle drawer of her desk, she took out a gold pen-and-pencil set and a few other snippets of memorabilia. She snapped the brief-case shut, slung her purse over one shoulder and picked up a planter of German ivy with her free hand. Cole stepped out into the hall; there was no sign of the receptionist, Warren or anybody else. No one was witness to the last time Cole Jameson ever graced the halls of Fawcett and Lloyd, Inc.

When she got home, the first thing Cole did was pour herself a celebratory glass of wine and utter a toast to the most outrageously spontaneous act she had ever committed. By now, someone would have noticed her disappearance, and as word spread everyone would probably conclude she'd gone off the deep end. But she'd never felt saner in her life.

Cole padded into the living room with her glass of wine and sprawled expansively across the sofa. Honestly, silk toilet paper for the *nouveau riche* tush! She'd always known advertising was capable of achieving low levels, but there were limits. Tomorrow she would sit down and pen her letter of resignation, which Alastair Fawcett would no doubt accept with great alacrity. A woman in the firm had always stuck in his antiquated craw, anyway.

She took another sip of wine and nearly spit it across the room. Imbibing at ten-thirty in the morning really wasn't much fun. Cole deposited the goblet on the coffee table and lay back on a pillow.

So now she had the rest of her life ahead of her to do whatever she wanted. No more moribund bosses, no more temperamental product managers, no more deadlines or breakfast meetings...no more paychecks. Suddenly, a tear appeared quite inappropriately on Cole's cheek. She brushed it away with a hasty swipe wondering what was the matter with her. There were other jobs, and advertising wasn't all that bad. Working for Fawcett and Lloyd had simply begun to grate on her lately, especially since she'd come back from Paris. Or, to be more accurate, since she and Adam had said their goodbyes.

Ever since then, nothing seemed to please her. Nothing could fill her days to the exclusion of her memories of Adam, and nothing filled the horrible, empty nights.

It had been Cole's decision that she and Adam not see each other for the short time he had left in Philadelphia; there was no point. The only good that had come out of all this, she'd decided, was that she now had Adam as a lifelong friend. In a few years she'd be able to see him and— Oh, hell! Who was she trying to kid? She could never content herself to view him as a friend, not after all they'd shared.

Yet, no matter how she looked at it—and she had looked at it every which way—there were no bonds to tie the two of them across an ocean and two continents. Adam had his commitments; she had hers—

Wait a minute! What commitments did she have now? None. She could do whatever she wanted. *So think, Cole,* she told herself. *What do you want to do?* While she struggled with the quandary, Cole's eyes were drawn slowly and irrevocably toward the wooden carving of the Haitian woman.

Her thoughts drifted back to the remote village where the woman had lived. She recalled the primitive but outstanding carvings the woman's husband had done, works of art virtually unknown outside the village. Surely there were countless people like him all over the world; people who, with the right encouragement and guidance, could expand their market and reap rewards for their artistry. All they needed was someone to show them the way, to open the right doors.

Cole's mind raced with possibilities and practicalities. She had enough working capital to get an import business started; she'd been investing precisely ten percent of her monthly salary in blue-chip stocks for years. Whatever else she needed in the way of funds could be borrowed, or she could search out philanthropists in need of a cause. She had the marketing expertise, contacts in the business world, a good head for figures. . . .

Why not? Ecuador was as good a place to start as any.

After several miles of productive pacing, Cole decided once and for all what she wanted to do. She wanted to get to Twin Elms right away. No point in calling Adam ahead of time. This morning, she needed the psychological edge of catching him off guard. She picked up the wood carving on her way out.

As she headed for the Torrie mansion, Cole's mind whirled hopelessly. Somehow she knew, though, that when the time came the right words would come out. She had never been more sure of anything in her life, except that she still loved Adam with every fiber of her being. She drove as quickly as she dared, her heart puttering like an outboard motor as she eased her car into the circular drive.

The security guard recognized her at once. "Mornin', Ms Jameson."

"Good morning, Jack. Is Adam at home?"

"Why, yes, I do believe he is. You might try the greenhouse. Do you know how to get there?"

"Yes, thank you," Cole answered, itching to be off.

"Okay, then, just lemme give you this security tag that lets you have free access to the house."

Cole waited for what seemed like hours as the guard entered her name and time of arrival in his ledger then fiddled with the tag's clip before finally handing it to her. She thanked him and drove off to park the car. Clutching the carving in one hand, she flew to the front doors where an overly solicitous guide let her in and insisted on showing her the way to the greenhouse, moving at a snail's pace. But at least he was home!

At the last leg of her journey, Cole was abandoned to pick her own way through the bougainvillea, strangler figs and giant philodendrons. She felt kinship with Stanley in his search for Livingstone. All she lacked was a machete and a troop of natives.

The gazebo was shut tight. Cole knocked twice and held her breath. At last the door opened and there was Adam, tall and dark and green-eyed, wearing nothing but a pair of faded corduroys. He looked so good!

"Cole!" he uttered in surprise.

"Hi! Can you spare a few minutes for a friend?"

"Of course." He stepped back to let her in. "Is something wrong?"

"No, not at all." Cole's body felt all warm and tingly just being near the only man who mattered in her life, especially here in his private little domain. Her eyes flickered over the eclectic decor that was such an accurate reflection of its owner. Books on every subject imaginable filled numerous shelves, clothes in casual disarray lay here and there, mementos of special places were everywhere. Her heart took a quantum leap when she saw the photo of them and *Stargrazer II* on his bedside table.

Adam noticed the carving in her hand. "Why'd you bring the statue with you? I hope you didn't plan on giving it to me because you think you need an excuse to be here."

Cole turned around to look up at him. "No, she's just my backup."

"Cole, you're being obscure. Why don't you sit down and tell me what's on your mind?"

She took a seat at the small table, which was covered with notebooks and medical journals. "Do you remember the first time you saw this carving, Adam?" Her adrenaline was flowing so fast that her voice came out a trifle high. Even ballooning didn't have this effect on her.

Grinning, he said, "How could I forget? That was the time I had to invite myself in for coffee, and you were plast—"

"Right, right," she said, cutting off his superfluous elaboration. "Well, this carving has given me an idea. I'm going to start my own import business of third-world handicrafts."

An expression that strongly resembled wistfulness crossed Adam's features. "That's a noble ambition. I wish you luck." He reached across the table and touched Cole's fingers. "I'm sure you'll do well no matter what direction you take in your life."

"Thanks," she replied evenly. "I thought I'd establish my business in Philadelphia and export from wherever I'm living."

It took a moment for her meaning to get through. When Adam let out a sigh of exasperation Cole knew it had sunk in, but she wasn't about to get discouraged yet. "We've been this route before, Cole," he said.

"Wouldn't you want me to be near you in Ecuador?" she intoned softly.

He slid his chair closer to her and moved his hand along her arm. "Of course, I'd love to have you with me, but what I want is not the issue here. You already have a successful career, a good life. You can't just throw everything away on a whim, no matter how good your intentions."

Cole gave him a Cheshire grin. "I'm afraid it's not exactly a whim. It's more like the only career option I have right now." She went on to relate what had happened that morning.

Adam, far from disapproving of her impulsive behavior, laughed heartily. "Scented silk toilet paper! I don't believe it! Cole, what you did was very courageous, if foolhardy. You never cease to amaze me with what you're capable of doing."

"I never intend to cease amazing you," she said, capturing his strong brown hand and bringing it to her lips. "So now, you see, I don't have anything to keep me here anymore."

Adam regarded her silently for a moment. Cole noticed he looked tired. The lines on his face were carved deeper than ever; there were shadows beneath his eyes and weariness in the set of his shoulders. And there was sadness in his face as well.

"Don't you realize we'd hardly ever see each other? I have to put in long days, and I'd be lucky even to get Christmas off."

Cole had arrived prepared for arguments. "I know," she said, "but I'll be working long hours, too. First of all, I'll need to clear my work with the government officials, whom I understand are expert bureaucrats. Then I'd have to win the confidence of the village officials and locate suitable interpreters until I can learn the dialects myself. Then there's the actual setting up of workshops, training programs, locating supplies of materials, not to mention the correspondence involved in developing an outside market . . ." Her voice trailed off when she saw Adam's expression grow thoughtful.

"If we're both going to be working so hard, what's the point?"

"The point is, my dear man, that each of us still needs to eat dinner, even if it's at midnight. And each of us needs to sleep, even if it's only for five hours a night. We can do those things together, can't we?" Cole walked her fingers along his arm. "Then, in a few years, when you're ready for another break, we could do some traveling, maybe a little ballooning . . ."

She looked up and their eyes locked. Love flowed between them like a rain-swelled river. Cole scarcely dared breathe as she watched Adam's pulse beat a steady rhythm in his neck.

"Basically, I think your idea is a sound one," he said at last. "But I do have one problem with it."

Cole dropped her head to the table in sheer frustration. Negotiating with this man was like bargaining with the devil. "What's the problem?" she asked, lifting her head.

"I know what village officials can be like. They're understandably distrustful of foreigners with big ideas. I have to be very sure that they aren't going to be exploited by some fly-by-night, get-rich-quick schemes."

"What are you implying?" Cole asked, her eyes narrowing.

"Well, I'm going to require something from you in writing that guarantees you intend to stick it out, no matter what happens. After all, you're going to be building up a lot of people's hopes. I can't have you getting discouraged after a year and packing it in."

"I wouldn't do that! How could you even think such a thing?"

"All the same," Adam insisted, "if you expect me to be even remotely associated with your business, I think it's only right that you demonstrate your good faith."

"Fine!" she snapped. "What do you want me to sign?"

"A marriage certificate should do it."

Cole gulped with a throat that had suddenly gone bone dry. "A what?"

"It's as good a guarantee as any. If you're my wife, you won't be packing your things and going home. You'll already be home." Adam's voice was as impassive as if he was discussing an investment portfolio, but his eyes were glinting with pleasure.

Marriage. The word was still bouncing around in Cole's head like a squash ball. "You really want to marry me?" She'd never expected to get this far today.

"Yes. Do you want to marry me?"

Cole couldn't contain herself a minute longer. She leaped from her chair and deposited herself in Adam's lap. "Of course I want to marry you, you stubborn, bullheaded man!" She threw her arms around his neck and kissed him soundly. "But only if you're sure that's what it'll take to win over the village officials," she added drolly.

Adam laughed, that deep satisfying laugh she'd been in love with right from the start. "That's exactly what it'll take to win over the village officials." Then he kissed her, erasing painful memories and replacing them with the sweet undying promise of his love.

When he brought his lips from hers, Cole's expression grew serious. "There is one more item we have to discuss before we commit ourselves any further."

Adam raised one eyebrow. "Oh? What's that?"

"Children."

"Do you mean in the global sense?" Much to Cole's amazement, he didn't appear the least bit disturbed.

"No, specifically," she said.

"Okay." Adam grew thoughtful for a moment. "I think I'd like one of each, but it doesn't really matter."

Cole sat up. "What? Are you serious? What happened to your philosophy about starving children and dumping grain?"

"Well, I've been doing a lot of thinking about that, and I decided that if I ever got the chance, the best thing I could do is have kids of my own. There's always a chance that one of them might grow up to be a researcher and find a cure for some disease, or become president of the United States and find a political solution to world hunger." The corner of his mouth lifted in a grin. "Of course, they might grow up to be basket weavers, and that's okay, too. Who am I to interfere in their lives?"

Cole could feel tears of sheer joy welling in her eyes. "Do you think we'll be able to find a housekeeper-nanny from the village to help out with the kids while I'm starting my business?"

"I'm sure we can," Adam replied with quiet pride. "You want to have children right away?"

"We probably should. I'm thirty-one."

"Okay," replied Adam. "We'll start whenever you're ready."

Cole's gaze slid longingly to the bed covered with the colorful Navaho spread. Turning back to Adam, she murmured, "I think I'm ready right now."

What readers say about Harlequin Temptation . . .

One word is needed to describe the series Harlequin Temptation . . . "Exquisite." They are so sensual, passionate and beautifully written.

—H.D., Easton, PA

I'm always looking forward to the next month's Harlequin Temptation with a great deal of anticipation . . .

—M.B., Amarillo, TX

I'm so glad you now have Harlequin Temptation . . . the stories seem so real. They really stimulate my imagination!

—S.E.B., El Paso, TX

Names available on request.

Harlequin Temptation

COMING NEXT MONTH

#141 LOVE IN TANDEM Lynda Ward

When Meredith first ran into Brandt, they were both stunned by the impact. Of course, she *had* knocked him off his bicycle. But what happened between them later was no accident....

#142 NO PASSING FANCY Mary Jo Territo

O'Mara was a man with fantastic moves, but Jo was the woman to show him a thing or two more....

#143 BED AND BREAKFAST Kate McKenzie

When Leslie O'Neill moved into the quaint but chaotic Seaview Inn, she suspected her stay would be less than serene. Already she was wishing her charming host, Greg Austin, would offer her more than bed and breakfast....

#144 TWELVE ACROSS Barbara Delinsky

Leah hadn't planned on being stranded in Garrick's secluded cabin. But she had no more control over the storm outside than the one that raged within.